The Red Boat
(Le Bateau Rouge)

by

Allen Brookins-Brown

DORRANCE
PUBLISHING CO
EST. 1920
PITTSBURGH, PENNSYLVANIA 15222

Dorrance Publishing Co
701 Smithfield Street
Pittsburgh, PA 15222
Visit our website at *www.dorrancebookstore.com*

ISBN: 978-1-4809-0180-3
eISBN: 978-1-4809-0450-7

Table of Contents

Chapter 1

Paris, spring, nineteen-thirty-nine

The cortege slow-cadenced up the *Champs-Elysées* toward the *Arc de Triomphe.* Iron-rimmed wheels of the gun carriage bit the pavement with a constant rasp, punctuated by the clopping shoes of six gray Percherons. One of the black-plumed horses snorted and thrashed out as if to break loose, but the traces controlled him, and he resumed his measured plodding. Groomsmen from the noblest houses of France flanked the caisson bearing a flag-draped casket. A wreath of black magnolia leaves bound by wide gold sheaves rested on the tri-colored flag. Nestled within the wreath, a plumed hat of a Field Marshal of France reflected the past glory befitting the deceased's rank. The mournful tattoo of twelve kettledrums sounded the sadness felt by the entire nation.

Following the rolling catafalque were six pairs of uniformed nobles, astride equally noble gray stallions, being trailed by two rows of drummers, eight drummers to a row. At intervals, three carriages trailed.

In the first sat the President of France and his wife. In the second sat the Commander of the Legion of Honor, himself too superannuated and corpu-lent to ride a horse. In a third, closed carriage rode the Comtesse Blanche Everon du Plais, the Field Marshal's widow. Forty years his junior, she became his second wife after having been his mistress for a scandalous twelve years, which is why she was in the third carriage. Opposite her sat her confidant, Vivian de La Roche, Paris's foremost *ingenue* of the public stage and occa-sional Presidential private entertainer.

The Comtesse, now in the position of being the widow of a deceased icon and no longer entitled to enjoy the status conferred on a companion of a living icon, was slowly coming to realize the inevitable, and presently indistinct, changes about to occur. For the moment, though, she remained wistfully in a nostalgic haze. The faces of the people around her blurred, as did the plumed

1

horses and the stately sycamores lining the cortege path. Her fingers fluttered indecisively about her black lace collar and finally settled on the octagonal gold locket hanging from a ribbon about her neck.

She had debated with herself about the appropriateness of wearing the locket on this somber occasion, but because he had given it to her, she had decided it would do, but only after replacing its gold chain with a narrow length of black silk.

She recalled how years before, they stood before the window of *Jollier Maillot*, in the Sixteenth *Arrondisement*:

He took her hand as she gazed in at the shop's display.

She knew what she wanted. "I'd like that, dear Philippe."

"What?"

"C'est ca… the locket. The one behind the brooch. The gold one."

"On the gold chain?"

"Yes. The one on the chain."

"Wait here."

From the sidewalk, she watched the pantomime inside the shop: the clerk, attentive and nervous in the presence of a uniformed Field Marshal, gesturing to the window with his gloved hand; the Marshal nodding in affirmation; the glove deftly pinching the locket from its stand; the purchase; the obligatory bow and escort to the door.

He said nothing while staring into her features. His thick gray eyebrows gathered in supplication over his fierce eyes as he took her hands in his own and kissed first one and then the other and placed the locket over her head.

Wordlessly, they turned and walked towards Montmartre and their new life as one.

A sudden neighing, punctuated by a scatter of clopping hooves, dissolved the image. The cortege had reached the traffic circle of the *Arc de Triomphe* on its roundabout way to *le cimetiere de Montmartre*. As the carriage turned right onto *avenue Wagram*, the bells from *Sacre Coeur* tolled somberly.

*　　*　　*

A newspaper office, two weeks later

The paper's editor, Andre Daumier, only that morning returned from vacation, scanned the loose manuscripts on his desk, only glancing at some and casting them side, studying others, scribbling margin notes, and frequently spearing one onto a metal spindle. Presently he became fixed on a grainy photo. He drew out a Galois from a pack on his desk and drew the photo close. It depicted mourners at a *Montmartre* graveside. Five men, six women, suitably clad in mourning for the late Field Marshal of France: the president of the Republic, with his wife standing behind him, the president of the Legion of Honor, his wife, the president of the *Academie Francais*, his wife, the Comtesse Blanche Everon du Plais, a plenipotentiary from the late Field Marshal's province, his wife, the Field Marshal's successor, and an unidentified woman in a *cloche* hat. The lady mourners sat closest to the grave, the men standing behind. An uncaptioned lieutenant stood in attendance, the finger of one hand discreetly resting upon the widow's shoulder.

Andre alternately sipped at his bowl of coffee and drew on a *Galois* before suddenly tensing.

"*Merde,*" he muttered. He turned and shouted out, "Vernon! Vernon! *Ici!*

A harried young man in shirtsleeves bolted into the office, clutching a nest of newspaper proofs to his chest.

"Yes, *mon Pere?*"

"So, do you see anything strange about this photograph?"

"Which photograph, *mon pere?*"

"*That* one. The one with the President of the Republic!"

"Ah, yes. He is not holding an umbrella, and it is raining."

"Observant. But I was more interested in the people being rained on."

He shoved the paper to the cowed underling.

"Read the caption, please, Vernon." The enunciation of his son's name dripped with condescension.

The hapless young man began mumbling the names.

"Aloud, please." Vernon started to read the names again, this time in a barely audible voice.

"Now, my dear *imbecile fils,* do any of those names sound familiar?"

"Of course, almost all of them, including Vivian de La Roche, the most famous actress in all France."

"Ah, ha! Now we are reaching into the deep pot of gruel that was given you for a brain. Now, look, once again. Does the woman on the second from the left look like the most famous actress in all of France?"

"I... think ...I... see ...what ...you ...mean ...It looks like the President of France."

"Not *that* row, *stupid.* That *is* the President of France. It's the *front* row, with the six women, as anyone who has seen a theatre poster in the last five years would know."

"But the caption says…"

"Never mind the fucking caption. The *caption is wrong.*"

"But, how can that be?"

"I'll tell you how. Someone in that lousy socialist crowd down in composition reversed the fucking negative when it went into rotogravure."

"So, which of the other ladies is the *Comtesse?*"

"I don't know, but for now, the damage is done. Perhaps we can hope no one has read the paper and we can forget about it?" Andre Daumier shrugged and turned back to his editing, as the hapless son shrank from the room.

*   *   *

3

Chapter 2

Paris, the Marais, an apartment on rue Mahler, July fifteenth, nineteen-forty-two

Crouched on the bottom step, knees drawn up to her chin, she waited behind the heavy wooden door until the hammering stopped. Each blow had caused her to wince and clutch her hands more tightly around her knees. There followed coughing, guttural and spitting, then momentary silence. The sound of the phosphorous match head scratching and the smell of tobacco seeped into her silent refuge. In moments, jack-boots clomped down the *sens unique,* receding into silence. She brought her arms down and cautiously stood up and opened the door a crack. Seeing no one, she opened it still but a few centimeters more and peered out onto the narrow coble-stones. Assured that no one was about, she stood hanging out of the doorway, the view revealing shuttered mansards being struck by the morning sun's early rays blazing just above the tiled roof of the building across the way, not yet pushing its sphere into full view. A calico cat, the street's sole occupant, padded down the cobbles, seeking refuge where only the cat knew. As she turned to close the door, a wind-gust rattled the paper, one that had just been pummeled to the door. Reaching up, she tore it down. The sound of the nail pounding had drawn her down from the fourth floor. The Swastika emblem commanding the top of the page made her tremble and clutch it, tightly. She turned and hurried back up the stairs.

She-her name was Sarah Goldschmidt-was fourteen and lived with her father, Israel, retired from the French army and a proud bearer of the Legion of Honor for heroism in the First World War; her mother, Rosa; and two sisters and two brothers, the oldest being Sascha, just turning twenty-three on that very day.

She climbed the wooden stairs slowly, scanning the paper. From time to time she paused on a step, reading a line or two, her face melding perturbative perplexity. Reaching the top floor where the family lived, she went through the hallway and into the small living room where her father sat at a small oval table, holding his morning bowl of coffee. He looked up at her as she, her eyes still focusing on the paper, kicking the door closed with her foot.

"What's that you're holding, Sarah?

"I don't quite know what, father. It was tacked on to the outside door. It's got one of *their* nasty eagle things on it."

"Let me see it." He set the bowl on the table and reached to take the paper from her hand.

A voice came from down the hallway, "Who took my jacket?"

Rachel answered, "What jacket?" her face contorting back a conspiratorial smirk.

"My regular one; I need it for work."

"You mean that old brown thing that was worn out?"

He stood in the hallway door, his arm impatiently akimbo. She feigned nonchalance as she returned, "I didn't think you wanted it any more, since I..." she pulled a jacket from behind her skirt and flounced coquettishly toward him, holding the jacket to her front, "...I made a new one for you, silly; here, try it on."

"You brat, you!"

He took the jacket and worked it through his hands, examining it.

"The collar's fabulous, Rachel. Where did you find it?"

"I found it at Moishe's shop and I re-did the collar, myself. Happy Birthday, Sascha; you're an ancient twenty-three, now."

He moved toward her and hugged her in an embrace.

"Thanks, you're not such a brat, after all, Sarah. I'll do something nice for you for your *Bat Mitzvah*." He looked at her affectionately, his hand on her shoulder. His voice fell. "That is, if they'll still let us do them. They're cracking down all over and not just here in the *Marais*."

"I mustn't be late; it's my turn to open the shop."

He bussed his sister on the forehead, and, throwing the jacket over his arm, he bolted down the stairs and into the street.

Her smile fell to a questioning expression as she turned back from the doorway and saw her father turned sideways in his chair, his one arm holding the notice, dropped to his side, murmuring inaudibly.

"What's that, Papa?"

Before he could answer, Sascha pounced back into the room.

"My keys, my keys...to the print shop. I left them..."

Seeing the keys on a small table, he took them up and bounded out and down the stairs.

Israel looked over his coffee bowl at Sarah and quietly ordered, "I *said*, get your mother; if she's not awake, wake her up. This looks serious." He fluttered the paper in his hand and let his arm fall, staring dejectedly about the room. From outside, a crow shrieked and flapped off in his own world of smoking chimneys and gray slated roofs.

*   *   *

"It says 'tomorrow.' That must be some kind of a mistake, Israel."

"The German's don't *make* mistakes, my dear. Something tells me we must prepare."

"How will we move the *Pleyel*, Israel?"

"We won't. The notice says one hand-grip per adult. None for the children."

"*Surely* there must be some...mistake? Can't we have some of our own furniture? The *Pleyel*? Father worked at the factory."

He looked at her steadily and shook his head then clasped it between his hands as he planted his elbows on the table.

"But how will we do without furniture? Will they have some, they *must* have some provision for...."

He turned his head toward her and looked and got up and went to where she was standing and took her in his arms and said, "I think it's more serious than we may realize, my dear."

He turned away and went into the hallway.

She turned towards her daughter, her arms hanging dejectedly at her side,

"Sarah, I don't know what all this means but we must do what your father says. Get out some of your things, the best ones, and we'll go over them together, later. Right now I must begin cleaning the house. If someone moves in, we don't want them to think we are a bunch of gypsies living here. Maybe they will keep it up better for when we return after all this is over, if we leave it in good condition. Now go start getting things out to go through. I have all this dusting to do."

"Israel, should we take down the Mezuzah or leave it up?"

There was no answer. He had left.

Two hours later, she heard his footfalls on the stairway. They were slow, disconsolately sounding with deliberation on each step; not his usual springy bounds of expectation, bursting through the door extending a rose and sometimes, even a full bouquet or a chocolate.

She stood expectantly, her arms at her side after she heard him reach the landing-top. On the other side of the door, his reach for the door was portent with reluctance: he would have to explain the unexplainable and so he waited. Minutes went by. She stood, motionless, her body half-way turned to the door. She put the duster down and went to the door and opened it. He was there, sitting on the floor slumped against the wall, his knees drawn up, sobbing. She reached over and touched him on the shoulder.

"Come, Israel. It can't be as bad as all that. I'll make some tea. Come."

He stood up and looked at her.

"We must act like it's nothing, nothing, nothing at all. We mustn't upset the children." His voice, a raspy whisper, signaled his despair more than his words.

6

"I went to the mayor's office. Bernstein was there. You remember him? He was at Goldberg's funeral. He had an arm band on. One of *theirs*. We talked. In whispers. He couldn't help. He's *watched*. *All the time*. There's nothing we can do. I couldn't even get in to see the mayor."

He took off his hat and hung it on the wall and sat down in the chair, not speaking, looking about, dejectedly. She started to speak, but words would not come.

*   *   *

Paris, an apartment, July sixteenth, nineteen forty-two

The dim light from the window awakened Vivian de la Roche. She stirred about and reached out to stroke the marmalade cat, pacing her front paws across its mistress's bosom. It was the morning hunger ritual, the cat having slept fitfully through the night, awakening once when the German staff car had screeched to a halt and its doors had slammed and its occupants had clopped nosily-the Germans never did anything quietly-into the *avenue Salengre* building and, from two floors below, had hustled the Rubenstein family from their apartment onto the pavement, the mother sobbing, the dog barking until a shot rang out, and the barking stopped with a pathetic yelp and the children of mixed ages crying, the tail-gate of the small truck that had followed the staff car slammed shut and both vehicles belched off into the night, the muffled cries of the children still audible to any who were awake and the dog bleeding to death on the paving below. The cat had been awakened earlier or later, unknowable-except to the cat, which-by a letter being slipped through the narrow letter drop in the hallway door. The cat had leapt down from the bed and had gone to the door and given an exploratory sniff to the envelope and had returned to the comfort of the bed, in complete stealth, as cats are wont to do, until its hunger demanded it activate its food source, who but minutes before, was sound asleep. Later Vivian de la Roche would read the letter.

It bore the date of July 15, 1942:

Dearest Vivian,

Things are growing tense here in the Marais and already two families have disappeared from the block. As you know the theatre has been closed for weeks and the Boche won't let any of us perform at a new venue (Because, as I learned, I am "Jewish").

I found that my dear Philippe was "Jewish" when the Boche posted a listing at the end of our street! He fought for France and his father fought for France and now, all of a sudden, in the grave, he's Jewish! And myself? Raised Catholic. Christened at Notre Dame! Perhaps I am unduly stressed and all this will be for naught, but tomorrow I will go to Gare Lyon and hop a train for Aix en Province.

I will write when I have a new address. If I find work there, I'll let you know and perhaps you can join me.

Fondly, B E D

*   *   *

Paris, the Rail Station, Lyon, July sixteenth, nineteen forty-two

"Deux café noire"

"Auch, mich."

"I already ordered for us both, *duckmauser.*"

The exchange was between *SS Oberleutnant* Gernot Burkheiser and *SS Unterleutnant* Rudolph Geisinger, sitting at ease at the station *Kaffeekonditorei* located at the terminal of the rail tracks. Their table faced the rail platform and gave a prospect of all the doors leading from the station ticket office and waiting room. Close by, it's cobalt blue locomotive panting impatiently, was *Le Tren Bleu,* a deluxe train, that would carry passengers, those few who had the money and the all important travel permits to the coastal Mediterranean resorts. Now, the passenger lists were heavily favored toward wounded German soldiers, arms in slings, on crutches, being sent for rehabilitation.

"Did I tell you I had new orders, to the Berchesgarten where *Reichsführer SS* Himmler has a chalet?" the *Oberleutnant* volunteered.

"Gott! That is *wünderschön!* What kind of duty?"

"Some kind of security, I suppose. It may be a promotion."

"You should drop a card to uncle Ringshoffer. He's got pull, somehow, through that shit he was in Munich in the *Putsch* when he took a bullet meant for the Führer. That set him up for life. The Führer always rewards people loyal to him. He is a model for all of us, really. Starting out as a Corporal in the First War, and now look how far he's come!"

"How long do you think the war will last, Gernot?", Geisinger asked, using the familiar "du" in addressing his superior because, in fact, they were second cousins and had gone to gymnasium together a four short years before in Munich.

"The Führer says that with the new secret weapons we should be done with the Ruskies 'any time soon'."

"I hope he is more right than *Der Dicke** was about our beloved Berlin never being bombed," Geisinger rejoined, referring to the Corpulent Nazi Field Marshall Hermann Goering.

He continued, "Remember Schmeltzer, the kid who did the pole vault and won all the ribbons in the *Jugend?* My mother met his mother at the KDW and said that when they got back from a week in Helgoland-his dad is richer than a skunk with I G Farben connections-they found the entire block just off

---

*   A popular pejorative among Germans for corpulent Field Marshal Goering, Chief of the *Luftwaffe,* who had bragged that Berlin would never be bombed.

Unter den Linden bombed completely to shit, I mean she said it was completely gone, no walls, just rubble. And no mention in the *Tagblat*."

"So, maybe she was delirious. I mean, if it didn't make it into the *Tagblat*, that means it didn't happen?"

"Try telling that to Schmelzer. They are living in a basement left by some Jews way out in Potsdam with *Strassenbahnen* that go every month or so it seems."

The two finished their coffees and sat, legs outstretched, eyeing train passengers hurrying toward the train platforms.

"Oh, look... at... *her!*" Burkheiser remarked, drawing in a deep breath, as she come toward them.

"Those legs. That dress!"

"I'd sure like to....She looks.....familiar! Where have I seen her? You've seen her, too."

"Fantastic *Zitzen!* How'd you like to nestle between...*Gott im Himmel* She's the Cabaret star...er...what's her name?"

" Du Plais! Blanche Everon Du Plais!", Gernot volunteered.

"Say...Isn't she a Jew. Yes!"

The two sprang from the table and intercepted her as she was about to pass by.

"*Fraulein. Eine Moment, bitte!*"

*   *   *

Paris, the Fourth arrondissement, early morning, July sixteenth, nineteen forty-two

Street vendors were laying out their shellfish, crabs, broccolis and breads taken just moments before from the oven-as the police vans and municipal buses stormed down *rue Rivoli* and, from the opposite direction, *rue St. Antoine*. Tailgates slammed down and French regional police dismounted, their boots clopping the paving blocks of the narrow *Marais* streets: the two blocks off *Barbette*, the five blocks off *rue de roi de Sicile*, *rue Mahler* and one block each of *rues Elzevir* and *Saint-Diene*.

Rifle butts crescendo against doors until they were either opened or they gave way to this harsh reasoning and families were pushed and shoved down the narrow streets and into the awaiting public transit buses. These unfortunates were the recalcitrant, those who had not responded to a more docile *tourisme* parade a week before, when some of the residents of the streets were given an hour to collect enough belongings to fit into one suit-case per family. The non-resident workers were not given such courtesy. They were assured by their fellow Frenchmen supervising the loading that they would be provided for. Not a few believed the fiction. Shouts from the transported wafted upwards from the cloud-shrouded narrow streets:

"I will write."

"I will be back for Israel's *Bar Mitzvah!*"

"The cat must go to the doctor next Monday!"

"The guards are French; we'll be all right!"

"Tell the children to study hard!"

The loading of the cumbersome public transport buses funeral black, all continued and, the engines revving up and the macabre procession wheeling the human cargo onto their first road to eternity. Dark clouds, gathering all morning, moved against the sun, blocking out the sorrow below.

Within the buses, whisperings: *"Val d'Hiv." "Drancy."*

Isaiah Goldschmidt, sitting at the end of the bus, stared upward at the home he would never see again. He felt in his pocket. He had forgotten to give his employer his keys to the shop and he worried.

Cringing under the mansard roof of Goldschmidt's family apartment, his sister, Sarah, nine years younger than her brother, took shallow breaths in hopes that she would not be discovered. She had adored him and had executed the petit-point around the jacket she had given him for *Hanukkah.* Her parents and other siblings were hidden within the bus confines. A week before, after having been advised by the local Jewish leaders that the French were not like the Germans and that they would be given valuable work in a relocation center to the north, at *Drancy,* she had watched as the mother packed all the family necessities.

"They will probably have a store there, won't they, Israel?" On the day they were to assemble, she was the last in line as the family trooped down the stairs and into the street. When she reached the door, she silently pushed it closed behind them and sank to the floor, terrified. Minutes passed as she slowly steeled herself and crept back up three flights. Lying flat on the planked attic floor, watching through a window the procession of the transportees, she looked with close interest as a tall SS officer, standing in studied arrogant profile, one arm akimbo, observed the loading. The distance was not great so she could view him as she concentrated on his features. Her brother had been the first to climb into the bus-the last of a trail of twelve public transport vehicles. She saw him through the large glass window, staring upward, anxiously-before the officer snapped his riding crop against his palm and two French policemen climbed aboard. The door closed and the mordant parade wheeled down the narrow *rue Sicile.* The officer climbed into a motorcycle sidecar and passed under her view, his jaw jutting into the rising sun. She lay prone, staring after him, burning his image into her memory for years to come. Months and years later she would awake from the nightmare which, at this very moment was unfolding.

*　　*　　*

Drancy Deportation Center, northeast of Paris, July sixteenth, nineteen forty-two

The buses rumbled by him as the black-uniformed Corporal signaled them to continue down the road within the barbed-wire enclave. The buses, fifty, from all parts of Paris, belched diesel fumes as they pulled up behind one another. Their human gatherings were from a general street round-up, markets, railway stations and a particular area, the *Marais* or "Jewish Quarter". The windows were filled with anxiety ridden faces-on this particular day, and for many days previous, middle class Jews being sent to what the Nazis euphemistically termed "relocation centers."

Major August Friedlander, on loan from the *Reichsministarium von Kultur* in Paris, and a specific assignment to the *Louvre,* attended to his duties diligently, those being the supervision of sorting out the contents of the suit-cases being cynically allowed the deportees upon evacuating their apartments.

Later in the relocation process, the fiction of permitted possessions would be extended for the entire journey to various concentration camps, where, only then would they be separated from their property.

It was August Friedlander's first day on his assignment, and he watched with detachment as the doors opened and the human cargo was ordered out. The guards at the end of each bus held clip boards and checked off names. As names were shouted out, the forced tourists jumped down, some holding babies in arms, others carrying massive leather suitcases. One elderly man wore a Legion of Honor ribbon in his lapel buttonhole. Most of the men wore double-breasted suits, the ladies their best calf length dresses, the fashion of the mid-1930s; all could have been arriving for a fashionable soirée on *Avenue Foch*. Unfortunately, today's soirée would end many days and miles away; so would the lives of the hapless citizens. Guards would randomly strike across the neck or buttocks to encourage quick movement to the confinement area. Occasionally, a shot would ring out, revealing a lack of speed by one of the new residents.

Friedlander observed the discharge of the most recent cargo and made suggestions to the captain in charge that the busses should not be driven forward into a dead-end position, requiring tedious backing up by the busses once they had been emptied and requiring the entire line to back up in preparation for the return journey. Friedlander directed a circular pattern for the vehicles so that once they entered they would be headed in the return direction once they had been emptied.

Having observed the reception procedure, Friedlander continued on to his principle duties, that of "conserving" personal valuables for the Third Reich. He turned and walked toward the former race track. Inside the cobble-stoned interior, he watched some of the new "guests," a sarcastic term he snidely assigned to the unfortunate arrivals as they trundled railroad baggage carts into a walled utility space commandeered for the purpose. He ordered the bags and suitcases placed in orderly rows, against the walls.

"You, put ten of those bags on the table and you, soldier of the Reich, open each one and remove the clothing, one by one. Check the pockets for coins and other valuables. All clothing will be sorted and placed in separate, like piles, shoes, shirts, skirts, suit coats."

Friedlander looked about to see if his orders were being understood and, as they apparently were, he continued,

"All jewelry, watches and chains and other valuables will be brought to my table here. You will be searched at the end of the duty. Anyone unlawfully removing valuables will be shot. Now, hop to it, Heil Hitler."

The soldiers rejoined, with a lusty, "Heil Hitler!"

Friedlander watched as the troops set to work. The day was hot, and he reached for his canteen and gulped down several draughts before propping his boots up on the table. Two hours went by.

Friedlander became pensive. Boredom was not his game. Was it worth his time to sort out mere baubles, trinkets, and mementos in this rustic enclave, a former racetrack garage? He thought not.

Three more hours passed. One suit-case was filled and another one brought before him to ingest the bibelots ("Bibelots of the Damned" a film title, perhaps, that he might one day write, Friedlander mused). A Star of David-was she wearing this for her bat mitzvah photo? Jeweled dancing pumps, a handful of lockets, all once lovingly taken from satin lined boxes, tenderly fondled by grandmothers, mothers, newly-betrothed, sometimes with the strains of love-enticing music at a Parisian *Le Bal* but now unceremoniously flung onto the pile to be "conserved" by dismounting stones and tossing the gold remainders into the melting pots, perhaps within the simultaneous hour of their owners being turned to ash in the ovens of Dachau or Belsenhausen?

And a fifth hour. Friedlander rankled. There were furnishings, tapestries, candelabra from Tsar's palaces, *Louis Seize* settees, items of great value, from museums and mansions and chateaus of the rich; but here he was slumming about with used clothing and trinkets. Frustration boiled within. He would send a post card to his uncle Heinrich to see about a posting elsewhere.

At the sixth hour, Friedlander ordered the soldiers to return to their barrack. Before him lay suitcases opened on the brick stable floor. In one were pocket watches, in another, necklaces. Others held ladies' lockets and neckpieces. He knelt down and randomly picked up a watch, examined it, put it back, picked another treasure out of the ladies' conglomeration; then another. This one, a gold locket. Octagonal; he held it in his hand and turned it over, examining the filigreed designs. Pushing a button on the side, it sprang open. The uniformed French officer's photo drew his attention. It interested him. He wondered who the officer might have been. And the lady whose neck it had once adorned. Friedlander put the octagonal locket in his tunic pocket and went toward his own quarters, pondering the possibilities that had just at the preceding moments been put before him. As he passed by the piles of discarded "guest" clothing, some still odeuered of their former wearers, he noticed a corduroy jacket and matching trousers that appeared to be new. He leaned down and picked them up, first the jacket, which he held out at arm's length, checking the size. Its collar had been carefully crafted in needlepoint in gray and black, not ostentatious. He liked it and threw it and the companion trousers over his arm, not knowing why but thinking they might come in handy one day. The Star of David sewn into the coat pocket he could do without. The keys that he found in the trousers he tossed aside, muttering "He won't be opening any doors where he's going."

*　　*　　*

Chapter 3

Paris, Saint-Denis, the office of the Mayor, nineteen-forty-four

As she was led into the office, the mayor arose from his desk and approached her solicitously, obsequiously. He offered her a seat, which she acknowledged with a bespoke air of superiority, befitting the widow of a Field Marshal of France.

"*Comtesse,* we are honored at your visit. And let me offer, at this late date, our condolences at the loss of your husband. It is a sad day for all of France."

"*Monsieur le maire,* your kindness is appreciated. These past months have not been easy for me, especially since there have been some difficulties with my dear, late husband's pension and the proper assignment of property for me. The mayor at my own department has been unable to help because of a revision of the records, and I was told by my cousin that since you have experience in these matters, you might be able to help."

"But, of course, Madame Field Marshal. I am honored and will do whatever I can. Just what is the problem?"

"There is an apartment that I am entitled to, not a specific apartment, you understand, but any apartment as part of my late husband's pension arrangement with France. The apartment was to be granted to him for his lifetime and, after that, for myself, for life. It is guaranteed, and I have seen a place, not extravagant, merely six rooms on the avenue *Salengre,* near *Sevres,* that will do. The Mayor is involved with a death in his family. You may have read of that in the paper, and that is why I need someone who can help immediately."

"But, I don't understand the details of the problem, with your documents, *Comtesse*. Where are they?"

"That's the problem. I don't know where they are. Six months ago, when I started to look for property, the military affairs office sent my identity card and my marriage certificate to the Field Marshal through the post. They weren't certified and have become lost somewhere in the postal system. I know this is absolutely ridiculous and, would you believe, the only documentation I have is in those things that were at my husband's office."

She smiled as she spoke with nonchalant cheerfulness, punctuating sentences with a wistful light giggle, at ease as though she were explaining to a garden club that a particular flower had not bloomed because of a strange anomaly of the weather.

"He took care of everything, always. In fact, the only evidence I have that I am anybody at all is in this newspaper clipping from the funeral."

She opened her purse, pulled out a clipping and hand fluttering, pushed it forward. "Here I am at the gravesite at *Montmartre* Cemetery. You can see, fortunately, that I am there, with the caption, '*Comtesse* Blanche Everon du Plais.'"

He took both her hands in his and said, "Comtesse, I want you to leave the matter completely with me."

"The description of the property is in this document."

"I will take care of everything. Rest assured that for the Field Marshal's memory, France will not forget."

She got up and made for the door, the mayor scampering ahead of her.

"When I am settled, *Monsieur le Maire,* you must come to lunch. You have been very kind."

The door closed behind her, and the mayor, still stunned in the afterglow, sat back down. To think, that he, Patrick Evian, son of a laborer from Lille had actually touched a personage of the same family as a Field Marshal of France! Surely, something grand would come of this? Yes? Perhaps? What would he wear for lunch? He picked up the phone. "I need Montmartre 81 97, please."

"Marcelle, it's your cousin, Patrick. I need a small favor. There is a lady of impeccable standing. I need you to arrange for an apartment."

*   *   *

Chapter 4

Roscoff, on the Breton coast, the dining room of l'Auberge Gaspard, late nineteen-fifties

Sargan Gaspard nervously clutched at the tablecloth as he unburdened himself of his secrets. Catherine sat across from him, her elbows on the table, her face — blank as a pantomime mask — resting in her palms. As his litany continued, her shoulders began to sag. Her hands fell, one to her wine glass and the other, limply, palm up, to the tablecloth. She rotated the stem of the glass, first in one complete circle to the right, then upon that completion, reversed the motion, staring an invisible spot on the table cloth. She was about to speak but held off when the hotel's waiter appeared and whisked away the *créme-brüler* cups. She looked nonplussed as she asked the waiter, "Tomorrow is your day off?"

"Yes, Madame."

"Thanks. Goodnight." "Goodnight, Madame Gaspard. Goodnight, Monsieur Gaspard." He turned and disappeared into the kitchen. She looked after him before turning back to Sargan."It seems you keep replaying the same song." She positioned each word as if she were a Zen monk mindfully dropping decorative stones in a monastery path. Sargan cringed but kept silent, hoping for a mercifully quick end to the scene. Silences likened seconds to hours. It wasn't so much the silences, per-se, that discomfited; it was their exquisite irregularity, punctuated by her panther-like breathing. They would end, finally, with a swift, ax-like verbal stroke, brilliant and unpredictable, shaming but justified. A master of timing, she sometimes focused her eyes on both her hands, rolling the glass stem between her palms, halting the motion to coincide with a falling of her voice. At times, she would fixedly stare at the glass stem as though Sargan were nowhere near and, at other times, as though he did not exist. Another twist of the dagger, she would suppose a novelist's scenario, describing events exactly snatched from their own marital history, and then would opine the novelist's treatments in various calculating manners, always with the novelist's portrayal of Sargan in decidedly disparaging-sometime obscene terms. In this last variation, she would lower her voice, addressing their situation in a colloquial third person, ethereal and more frightening because of its quiet intensity. At other times, she would recreate previous whipping conversations between the two, sometimes setting up Sargan as a target as she drummed out the pathetic details of his previous escapades. Tonight, she turned her back and looked out at the harbor crescent, lit by the occasional sweep of the lighthouse lamp. She began twisting the stem again with slow, precise turns that tendered a faint squeak. For Sargan, the sound was like a medieval rack. He imagined he could hear ropes tautening his limbs. He wished he could change places with someone, anyone, even a tortured medieval. He drummed a tattoo with his fingers, swiveling his neck right to left, as though viewing some distant place on the harbor reaches, never looking at her, *that would reveal more secrets, yet held, and hopefully never to be discovered, no, mustn't look her in the eye, eyes are the path to the mind and, no, never shall she see into his mind, never.* He had been through these scenes before and knew just about what to expect. Seconds passed like the regular spacing of thunderclaps in a summer storm.

"Don't you...?" she didn't finish the question, but spun the air with her hand, letting it fall to the table.

"It just happened, Catherine. What more can I say? It just happened. It just happened. If I could take it back, I would, Catherine. Fuck, if I could take it all back, but..."

"Taking back all the loose sperm you have shot all over the Brittany coast would take two of Monsieur LeBlanc's septic wagons." Her voice was quiet, measured, and almost emotionless. It held neither hatred nor contempt and, unfortunately for Sargan, neither did it hold love. The candle flickered as her words slowly bit the air.

"So, what is she going to do? Have it or not?"

"She's Catholic. She wants to have it."

"In a little town like this? There goes the mayor's job, Sargan."

"She wants to have it, but put it up for adoption."

"Grand. Simply *grand*, Sargan, *grand*." The words hissed out of her taut lips like a steam radiator.

She fell silent and looked past him to the harbor. Minutes passed. Then Sargan spoke.

"I don't know what to do. I thought the money..."

"*What* money, Sargan?" she asked, her voice spiked with incredulity.

"She said everything would be all right if..."

"If, what?"

"If I..." He hesitated, knotting the tablecloth more tightly in his fist.

"If you *what*?"

"Gave her the money."

"How much money, Sargan?"

"A lot."

"Sargan. How much money? *How much?*"

He hesitated, his eyes falling to the table, his fingers releasing and clutching the tablecloth. "Fifty-thousand francs."

"Fifty... Thousand... Francs!" She pronounced each word with leaden incredulity. "That's half of our savings. That's God knows how many rooms I've had to clean. All because you can't keep your cock..."

She fell silent and turned her body away from Sargan and again looked out onto the harbor. Minutes ticked past like drops from an icicle melting from an eve. She twisted her glass and turned back to Sargan, glaring.

He spoke. "Catherine, there are some other expenses, such as—,"

"Shut *up*. *I'm* thinking"

She glowered and drummed her fingers on the table, took a sip from her glass and leaned back in her seat and resumed her drumming.

"Sargan, I can see expenses such as the hospital, a doctor, a place for her to stay, but here's what we will do." Her words marched with the instructive finality of a banker calling in a note. Sargan sank back and cringed.

"We'll send her to *Quimper*, to my cousin's, until her time comes. In that way, when she begins to show, people won't figure things out. Knowing you, Sargan, people here will figure things out. That leaves one thing."

Sargan parted his lips as though to speak.

"No, Sargan. *I'm talking*. That leaves one thing. The problem of handing your baby over to strangers. I don't like that. You'll have to get her to agree to one thing."

And so it came to pass that before Joline began to show, she departed *Roscoff*, for the town of *Quimper*. When the baby arrived, he was christened Jean-Baptiste Gaspard in the nave of the cathedral in *Quimper*. After the christening he came to live with his father and the woman he believed to be his mother in *Roscoff*. And despite the storm that preceded his birth, Catherine grew to love him as her own. Time passed. Joline even returned to work at Sargan's office. On Sundays, she would come to the seawall at *Roscoff* and watch Jean-Baptiste look for sea creatures and clamber onto the red boat.

In time, though, Joline grew restless. She began to plan.

*   *   *

Chapter 5

Roscoff, a room at the Auberge Gaspard, a fall day in nineteen-sixty-four

Charles Edouard Dufresne turned his back to the dull sunrise as he opened a fresh roll of film. Three tripods, each supporting a time-lapse camera, stood like iron spiders at the windows of his second floor room at *l'Auberge Gaspard*. The lens of one camera was focused on a brownish stone lighthouse, a grim remnant of mid-nineteenth century marine architecture, which (he had learned and re-learned, the night before) emitted a tireless, tepid light that loped glumly from the harbor-front windows to the open sea and back again. The two other cameras took in the remainder of the town's antediluvian seawalls, black and forbidding, as well as the concrete German fortifications that had failed to repel the allied forces during the Second War years of 1939-1945. The cameras were set to capture their images every half hour. When the pictures were developed, they would meld into a single panoramic image. Dufresne, M.D., Ph.D. according to many, France's most august authority on marine biology, was in *Roscoff* to attend a weekend research conference. He was also indulging his fascination with light infraction as captured on film. To that end, he was enlisting the help of his nephew, Melville Saint Eustace , who lived in *Roscoff* with Dufresne's sister.

The seven-year-old, unused to early morning assignments, yawned. *"Mon oncle,* won't the light change when the tide comes in? Water reflects, you know and the sky, also. Out there, it looks like rain."

"Of course, but the cameras automatically adjust for that, Melville. It's the newest thing. Now, watch while I load the new film. If I'm delayed at my meetings, I want you to reload the cameras. A timer can go for only eight hours. After that, the film runs out and is automatically rewound."

He finished loading the new roll and, with a wax pencil, marked the exposed film canister with the date, time and *"la mer Roscoff"*. An instant later, one of the cameras clicked and whirred. Dufresne looked out to see what it had captured. In the early light, the receding tide, mottled with undulating patches of sunlight, continued to recede from the peaceful harbor. He wondered where those waters would be the next day and countless mornings after. Past the English Channel? Splashing the shores of Brazil? The scene offered Dufresne a peace not found in his apartment in the tumultuous sixth *arrondissment* of *Paris:* the screams of the gulls, swooping and diving crazily about; the murky sky merging on the distant horizon with the sea; the small boats, their tipped hulls awaiting their next flush of tidewater ten hours hence.

Another camera clicked and whirred. He watched absently as a man led a little boy up the stone harbor steps and to a small white Citroen van. It was early and only the two were on the beach. Dufresne watched as they got into the van and drove off. The third camera clicked.

He turned to his nephew. "There. They're all working. Now, I must hurry to catch my bus. Come. I'll leave my room key with Madame Gaspard. You'll tell my sister I will call her from *Rennes* when I arrive home tonight and I should return next week. Tell her not to go to any extra trouble for me."

A clock struck seven as they made their way down the steep stairs.

*　　　*　　　*

Jules Gaspard dangled his bare legs over the mossy outcroppings of the seawall. It was breakfast time and he was impatient with Roué who had not done his morning "business" in the sand. The puppy had fixated on a long-legged insect scurrying along the gray, foaming necklaces of the ebbing tide. When the puppy neared the steps below *l'Auberge Gaspard,* Jules decided he would follow.

Jules jumped down onto the moist sea floor and, losing his balance, fell forward on his hands and knees. He sprang up and brushed away the sticky sand. It would not please his mother if he came to the breakfast table with stains on his newly-laundered trousers. As he followed Roué's trail, he found other fresh footprints. They belonged, he knew, to Jean-Baptiste, his little brother, who frequently played barefoot along the arc of the harbor. That morning, Jean-Baptiste had been up before him. But he must have tired of the beach already and gone inside to eat his breakfast in their parents' hotel. Jean-Baptiste was five, almost half Jules' age and one-third the age of their older brother, Pierre. Jules earnestly and impossibly wanted to catch up in age to Pierre so that he could himself be the oldest brother. But, clearly, this would never happen and that, in his mind, was unfair, indeed. At least Pierre was gone, having left one evening without a word to anyone. That was the night the police had arrived. There had been a murmured conversation in the vestibule, ending with the door closing and the flashing lights of the police car vanishing over the hillock leading out of the town. No one in the family ever spoke of Pierre, which bewildered Jules and his sister, Irene. Jules tried asking straight out one morning at breakfast when his brother would be coming home. His father, startled, looked up from his newspaper and then squinted meanly at his wife. She immediately left the table and, sobbing, scurried into the kitchen. Irene and Jean-Baptiste remained silent as their father reached over and pinched Jules' shoulder. The man spoke in a tone they had never heard from him before.

"Don't ask questions about your brother, ever, *ever* again." They all stared as their father abruptly slammed down his paper and stood up, menacingly, arms stiffening at his sides, fists clenching open and shut, jaw clenching, then charging through the kitchen door.

Jules' sister Irene counted very much in Jules' life. She was older, fifteen. They shared a secret. Even though she said she was religious — she would push her chair back from the dining room table, throw the back of her hand against her forehead and moan that she needed to go to her room to pray because the Virgin was calling her — Of course, Jules knew she wasn't religious at all. She did not even stay in her room. On his own twilight excursions out of his bedroom window to watch the sea, he had often seen Irene making late-night departures from her bedroom's gable and once, he had discovered her in the garden house with the plumber's helper, Antoine Ranier, when she was supposed to be at catechism. The two were on the hard-plank floor. Antoine, his trousers at his ankles, was bending down to kiss her on the lips, but Irene noticed Jules and hissed him away.

Afterwards, Irene and Jules had struck a bargain. She would buy Jules a *glacée* once a week if he did not mention what she and Antoine were doing in the garden house. That was almost two years — and a hundred-and-seven *glacées* —ago. He kept news of her evening exits from her window to himself, hoping for more rewards.

But now none of that mattered as Jules followed the little footprints, farther apart than his own. "He must have been running," he thought. He followed them as they wound around the sailboats; all tilted on their sides in the mocha-colored sand, the boats that would slumber until the evening tide floated them free and covered their beds. The footprints turned toward a red, square-stern sailboat. Jules went close. The years had faded the boat's color from carmine to rust. He had never seen it put out to sea. He often wondered why such a nice little boat would stay in the harbor. Now he noticed another, larger set of footprints, cupped like open clamshells in the sand. The smaller trail merged with them and then disappeared as the larger prints dug deeper on their way to the granite steps of the seawall.

His attention was drawn to the happy yelps of Roué, the family pet, which appeared out of nowhere depositing a soggy water-sodden shoe at his feet, a sport shoe with a yellow stripe, like the one Jean-Baptiste had pestered his mother to buy him at the Saturday market. Roué wanted Jules to hold the shoe so he could tug on it, but Jules did not want to play. He was suddenly certain that his little brother had gone away, though he could not imagine why. Or, if alone.

✻   ✻   ✻

Catherine Gaspard set the table in the breakfast room of *l'Auberge Gaspard*. The room was narrow, three meters wide by eight, just large enough to fit in eight *petit déjeuner* tables. Three walls of textured gray plaster held bright yellow and blue *Quimper* pottery platters. At one time, the walls had been decorated with more subdued plates from a local potter, but after an impressive guest from New York, a decorator, had opined that the plates "didn't look French enough," Catherine Gaspard had replaced them. The fourth wall, floor-to-ceiling plate-glass framed the finger of a causeway pointing out into the Atlantic's heaving swells. Catherine looked up from the tables and watched the distant waves merge with a menacing pewter sky that predicted a late-morning storm. The insistent ringing of the chrome-plated plunge-bell on the concierge desk broke her brief reverie and drew her to the next room. A man in an overcoat stood waiting, his hat on the desk, his suitcase at his feet.

"*L'addition*, Madame?" he asked, referring to his bill.

"Certainly, *Monsieur* Perrigort. You will not be having breakfast?"

"*Non, Madame.*"

"Was your stay satisfactory?"

"Of course, Madame."

"Twenty-eight francs, *Monsieur*. Will you be taking the train or the bus?"

"Actually, I will take the bus to *Morlaix*. Then the train to *Rennes*. But first I must find someone. Do you know where I can locate Monsieur Alois Castaignet?"

Catherine checked the man's face to see if he were serious. Perhaps he was a relative, or a genealogist. "But of course, Monsieur. You go out the door and up the strand, to where there is a small passageway between the *frites* stand and the wine shop, opposite the lighthouse. Follow it up to the orphanage and go along the wall and you'll find him there. You'll find the rail bus comes to the same place."

"And is there a train later in the night?"

"No. Not until the next morning."

"Thank you."

He picked up his hat and suitcase and turned to the door that would lead him to the harbor crescent.

"What a strange request," thought Catherine as she returned to the breakfast room.

"Perhaps he's an aficionado of the resistance." She looked out of the plate glass wall, watching Monsieur Perrigort head down the harbor road. The tide was out, she noted and the sandy bottom of the sea lay littered with shells and other treasures that her weekend guests from Paris would eagerly gather.

Her eyes traveled the beach in search of Jean-Baptiste and his blue sailor shirt. Her youngest loved to collect the snail shells and crab legs and other fascinations that the sea's foaming mass brought in during the night. But now it was time for him to come in for his *croissant*. She couldn't see him from the breakfast room, so she went to the lobby door and out across the road to the low wall that overlooked the beach. She thought she might find him at the base of the wall where he and Roué, sometimes liked to dig. Her eyes traversed the beach, from the stone boat ramp that guided small craft down to the water and then along to the roadway. He wasn't at any of his usual play spots, not even the pedestal of the old lighthouse where he liked to watch tourists take their "We were there" photos.

The boy was nowhere to be seen. She could see his older brother, Jules, seated against the seawall with his knees drawn up watching Roué. Her eyes darted, zigzagging about the beach, from boat to boat.

The desk telephone in the hotel rang out through the open lobby door. Not wanting to take her eyes from the beach, she nevertheless ran back into the hotel. It was the grocer, offering artichokes. Oh, yes, she would take one box and some carrots, as well. She hung up quickly and hurried back outside to continue her search for Jean-Baptiste. From the sea came a clap of thunder. She looked out as the sun hid behind a looming cloud.

For the first time she noticed a small group of young people, much too far down the beach, hovering over a canvas-covered form. She scurried down the stone steps leading to the beach and kicked off her shoes and then started to run across the sand crying, "Jean-Baptiste!"

Catherine ran toward the knot of onlookers gathered in a rough circle around the canvas-covered form. She thought of her husband. *Where was Sargan? He should be with me now.* As she approached the group she recognized Melville, from the flower shop, his hands in his pockets. And Antoine, the plumber's apprentice, a cigarette drooping from his lips. Antoine simply stared at her, a quizzical look on his face, uncomprehending. *She was the boy's mother. How could Antoine be so uncaring?* Infuriated at the collective nonchalance, she pushed her way through to the form on the wet sand and fell to her knees, crying out, "Jean-Baptiste!" She pulled away the canvas covering to reveal a baby shark—dead, quite dead. A dead shark. Not her Jean-Baptiste. She collapsed into sobs and threw back her head. The young people dispersed, more afraid of her than curious about the Dead Sea monster. She sat back and drew her knees to her chin, weeping. A hand touched her shoulder.

Jules, his timid voice mingling with dejection, spoke, *"Maman,* will he return?"

"The shark is dead, my dear."

"Non, Maman. Jean-Baptiste."

"He can't be far. We will go look for him in the town. He's just wandered off. Come."

She got up and took Jules by the hand, heading him toward the stone stairs.

"But, *Maman*," the boy persisted.

"Hush, I must think where he could have gone. Maybe for a *glacée*. But, no, it is too early for the shop to be open." She recovered her shoes and took Jules's hand and led him up the steps. They crossed the roadway and began a wandering search of the village streets. They went everywhere Jean-Baptiste would know: the railroad station, the flower stalls and even the gate of the convent. They searched for an hour, finally returning to sit at the top of the same steps. Madame Gaspard's eyes traveled the contours of the shore, from the lighthouse to the causeway and back again and then around the tilted boats scattered on the beach.

"*Maman*, I know he was here, "Jules sighed. "See, his little foot prints go up to the red boat."

*   *   *

Tax inspector Jean Perrigort made his way along the harbor crescent until he found himself opposite the lighthouse at the far end of the strand. The gray storm that had paced the horizon was now nearly at the shore. A large blue and white *pommes frites* sign called out from his left. He walked up the narrow, cobbled street and along blocks of shops and homes-brutish granite Breton conformities, all, their windows uniformly trimmed in peeling white.

Beyond the last house, several walled gardens led his eye to a gloomy pebbled-stone construction, a four-story Gothic monument to religious militancy and orphaned children. Its blue-gray slate roof was punctuated with two rows of austere dormers that glowered out at the village beyond. The words, *Saint Agnes,* imbedded in faded gold. arched in cursive over the gate. Perrigort shuddered at the relentless, cold piety projected by the edifice. He made his way to the end of its wall and, turning his back to the sea, surveyed gray-green fields of artichokes and cabbages planted in rows that stretched out immeasurably into the mist.

Across the road, he mounted the concave steps leading up to le *Cimetiére de Sainte-Agnes* and pulled open the rusted gate. Inside the wall, he paused. A foghorn from the harbor sounded mournfully as the first splashes of expected rain began to fall. "Why should it sound just now, as I'm entering the home of the dead?" Snippets of poems invaded his mind. *"The last harbor..." "The harbor of Death...?"*

Methodically, he made his way down the rows of graves marked with their patriarchal crosses enameled in black or corroded to rust. Some stone monuments tilted at rakish angles of neglect. Presently, he came upon two graves, side by side. In the black marble of one shone the inscribed gold words *Alois Castaignet.* Next to him rested, *Renaud Penze, Hero of France.* Both graves sported funnel-shaped glass vases, one with dead flowers leaning out indifferently. The other contained discouragingly colored plastic imitations. Perrigort noted the date on the Castaignet tomb, which raised a question. He stood for a moment and then pulled out a small notebook from his overcoat pocket. He scribbled something and put the book away. He was done with this place.

He had taken only a few steps toward the entrance when the sound of an approaching motor caused him to quicken his pace.

He hastened past the rusted cemetery gate just as the autobus was coming to a halt. Hurrying down the age-worn stone steps, he was at the bus as its door opened. A heavy-set woman, a black umbrella hooked over her arm, a bouquet of plastic flowers clasped against her coat, lumbered downward, sighing at each step. As she reached the last step, her bouquet fell to the paving. Perrigort stooped to retrieve it, handing it to her.

"Oh. *Merci, Monsieur,*" she offered as she accepted the flowers and turned toward the gate. Perrigort climbed toward the driver and the door closed behind him. The vehicle belched exhaust and headed on down the road. Overhead, a clap of thunder sounded and the morning's constant drizzle turned torrential. The woman opened her umbrella and looked quizzically towards the bus, processing a recall, before turning and laboring toward the cemetery entrance.

*   *   *

In the nearby town of *Morlaix,* Joline waited for Sargan Gaspard, to quiet his exertions atop her. He was no different, she thought, from her husband, Serge, who had left her a year before forcing her to look for work. And now, another, animalistic part of her job. The two had met through a mutual acquaintance. Sargan often traveled to *Morlaix* to represent railroad workers with bodily injury suits against the *Societe national des chemins de fer Francais.* When the injury manifestation did not evoke sufficient pathos, Gaspard would refer the plaintiff to Joline's friend, a practitioner in *Morlaix,* who specialized in plaster casts which could be worn in the courtroom and removed in the privacy of the plaintiff's home. Sargan asked her at her interview in *Morlaix* if she knew how to type and how to keep quiet. She had nodded yes to both questions. She admitted to herself that she had, at first been attracted to him, the only successful attorney in Roscoff, the risk-taker with the busy eyebrows and the sunken cheeks that, despite his weary thirty-nine year-old eyes, triggered a maternal yearning. It was only six months before, after and evening of correcting clerical irregularities made by her predecessor, that they first ate together at the pizzeria and he had walked her back to her small apartment; only six months since he had held the vestibule door open and followed her in; six months since his hand had found her breasts and his tongue first entered her mouth; six months since her backward march to the elevator, her clumsy unlocking of the door and her falling back onto her couch, where, now, once again, he was done. She stared over the shoulder of his stilled body and then closed her eyes as he got up, wordlessly, dressed and headed for the door.

*   *   *

Jules Gaspard trudged up the stairs of his family's hotel. He took the steps slowly, tired from the day's anxieties and from being permitted to stay up an extra hour to greet his brother when he returned. But Jean-Baptiste had not returned and Jules's dejection now made the stairs, built in the hollow of the adjacent bedroom, seem steeper than on previous nights. His mother, her hand on hip, stood watching from below.

He wanted to stomp on each step in protest, but he didn't have the heart. He snuggled a tattered velour bunny to his chest, the one he and Jean-Baptiste had tussled over until, one day, Jean-Baptiste held only a pink-and-white ear and the unresisting body. He pouted at his mother as she withdrew and pulled the hall door shut. Just after, the automatic timer for the stairway light clicked off.

Jules was used to searching for the switch; countless times he had climbed the stairs so slowly that the light had turned itself off in the middle of his progress — the light that didn't like to wait for little boys who didn't want to go to bed.

When he reached the top of the stairs, he went into the bathroom and took the tub's stopper and pushed it into the drain before cranking open the tub's cold water tap. For a moment he watched the slow stream from the spigot, then stepped across the hall to the small room he shared with Jean-Baptiste. He began to undress, folding his clothes and hanging them on the straight-back chair, as his mother insisted.

When he had folded his undershirt and placed it on the chair back, he went to the bathroom and shut off the water. The tub was but a quarter full; the water ran slowly in the older parts of the village. He grabbed a sponge ducky from the soap dish and knelt down to soak it in the chilly water and then he threw it against the tub side and watched it slowly come to the surface of the gentle waves.

He stared, waiting and listening for the helpful closing of the squeaky living room door below. When it finally sounded, he splashed the water theatrically for a few minutes; then he pulled the stopper out of the drain. He called goodnight to his mother and slipped on his nightwear and stepped across to his bedroom and lay down. But sleep was impossible. He turned on his side and saw the single eye of Jean-Baptiste's toy tiger staring from his brother's bed. When the lighthouse's sweep hit the room it would make the tiger's eye glisten. Jules thought the light in the tiger's eye made it look angry, as though Jean-Baptiste's absence was Jules's fault.

The other toys, too, seemed upset. They lay scattered about on the floor: tumbled alphabet blocks; a wheeled elephant, with a tow-string, tipped on its side; a wooden locomotive still missing the passenger cars that the tide had washed away when Jules had forgotten them on the beach. Jules wondered if he would ever have to keep his promise to buy his brother new cars. *What if Jean-Baptiste never came home? Pierre had never returned. Would his father pinch him again if he asked at breakfast about Jean-Baptiste?*

Jules continued to shift restlessly about, wondering at the strangeness of his brother's disappearance. How strange it seemed that his parents had refused to call the police the way they had when Pierre ran off and when Irene, one night, had missed her curfew. It was strange that the toys in the bedroom were now in such disarray, for it was Jean-Baptiste's custom before bath time to line them all up neatly under his bed, talking to each as he did so. Jules pulled the coverlet over his shoulder and tried once more to sleep. The foghorn sounded and the harbor light glanced its soft glow along the chimneys and shop fronts and into the seaside rooms of the hotel.

Still, sleep evaded him. Half-dreaming, he worried that if his little brother came home later that night and couldn't get in, he would die in the claws of the monster that their sister told them always lurked in the harbor's roils, always waiting for little boys who misbehaved. So, he got out of bed and went to the window and crawled out upon the slanted slate roof. The day's rain had wetted it and the wetness seeped through his sleeper and was cold. But he didn't care; he felt good, now that he could be the first to see his brother's return, so he pulled his knees up under his chin and waited.

If I wait here, I'll be the first to see him and then I can run and tell Maman. He won't stay away too long because he likes to play on the beach and there isn't another beach like this one in the wide, wide world. I know that for a fact. Besides, he wouldn't go away and leave his toys behind.

If I could go to the moon, I could see where Jean-Baptiste is and fly down and lead him home. First I must learn to fly. It would take at least an hour to get to the moon. I could start at the lighthouse. I'd need a ladder for that and then I'd go to the nearest cloud. I'd wait for one of the low ones and it would carry me up to the higher ones and then up to the moon and, maybe, I could find people on the moon and if they have puppies, too, they could tell me if they have a puppy like Roué and then, after I find Jean-Baptiste, we'll both climb down and I can go to university and become a doctor and use big words like the doctor who comes to the hotel and takes pictures and—

Jules looked up at the dark-velvet sky; the moon, a half-circle of mystery that suddenly hid itself behind the clouds. He grew irritated at the moon for hiding because that made it dark and if his brother came along, he might not be able to see him.

He heard the approach of a lorry. As it passed below, its tires hissed on the rain-wetted macadam. The sluicing of the tires, overlaid with the purr of the engine, slowly diminished as the vehicle traveled the arc of the road, leaving only the sounds of the harbor waters slapping against the anchored boats. The clouds pushed on in their purposeless journey and the moon came out as Jules, half-asleep, half-awake, consumed by thoughts of picnics, birthday fetes, a pet rabbit, the day the teeter-totter broke at friary school, all melding into pleasant haziness.

His thoughts wearied and he continued to nod off, but again rousing himself, positive Jean-Baptiste would return and he had promised himself he would welcome him back and would let him play with his toy soldiers and toy Peugeot and look into his treasure box and he would never, absolutely never play tricks on him again. But he soon grew very tired and drifted off to sleep.

Above, the clouds continued their dance with the moon before dissipating into the vagary of the night sky. Inside the bedroom, the toy tiger's one glass eye gazed across the empty beds. Out in the small harbor, the red boat pulled at its mooring, impatient to be free.

Chapter 6

The cemetery in Roscoff, a day in nineteen-sixty-four

At the cemetery gate, Louise Vernet braced her umbrella against the rain, lumbering her girth up the five steps and began to pace slowly down the graven aisles, her head pivoting right and left, her eyes searching.

At the far corner of the graveyard she came upon what she sought. She knelt down behind a large marker and lifted a rock. Underneath, the rotted remains of a cardboard shoe-box, disintegrated, its contents worm-holed, musty and rotted. She wormed her palm back and forth across the outline of the box but not finding what she had been seeking.

Standing erect, she leaned against the marker, her own height, and dropped her arms to her sides, sobbing. Then, recovering her aplomb, she made her way back, far down the pathway. She stopped at a black marker, *Alois Castaignet*. And nearby, *Renaud Penze*.

A storm crossed her face as she reached into her bouquet of artificial flowers. She pulled half the stems from the wrapping and flung them down on the Castaignet grave. The remaining plastic blossoms she tossed carelessly onto the graven letters *Renauld Penze*. Then she fumbled with her undergarments and squatted down, straddling the Castaignet grave. Under the wobbly umbrella, the warm stream steamed against the cold ground. When she finished, she rose and adjusted her clothes.

Her mouth twisted into a feral sneer. She whispered a low, guttural, "Happy birthday, *Monsieur Traitre.*" The rain pushed in sheets against her umbrella as she lumbered towards the gate. *Nineteen years is a long time. I wonder if anyone else will remember?* She went out the gate and crossed the road and walked along the orphanage's stone wall towards the center of town.

She gave scant notice of the crèche-bound Virgin Mary and the Latin inscription over the Virgin's halo. The lettering, exposed to two centuries of

Brittany's harsh coastal gales and neglected in a decades-old Catholic malaise, was barely legible.

Continuing in the direction of the village center, she eventually took a path that passed between walled gardens before reaching the seawall. Once there, she paused to gaze out at the gray Atlantic, undulating and foaming. After a moment, she turned toward the row of houses fronting the harbor, some of which had not yet been built when she had been sent away. Gray and oppressive, they marched with relentless congruency along the harbor frontage their, stone-block construction evoking the cold hearts of the villagers who betrayed her those many years past.

On her left, ahead, the lighthouse still stood, a brown ugly pile, seigniorial, stolid, a remainder of the *beaux arts*, as unattractive now as it was when it was erected in the 1870s, stone by stone, mason's epithet by mason's epithet.

Moving step-by-step, as though each required a separate motivational thought, she loitered along the harbor wall. Barely a meter high, it's purchase a full view of the harbor's taupe floor. She had strolled but ten or twenty meters when she looked down and saw it, half-embedded in the harbor sands: the weathered board with faded paint signaling *Les Fleurs Saint-Eustace*.

Stunned, she stood drawing in a deep breath as wartime memories flooded her mind.

*   *   *

*She hefted the planks down from the flower stall and lumbered them, one by one, to the side. Eight in all, each twenty centimeters wide: **LES FLEURS SAINT-EU-STACE** in art nouveau lettering entwined with tiny vines of violets. Once she finished taking down the eighth and last-which usually stuck in the frame holding the entire concern up-she began setting out the morning selections, which had been brought to Roscoff on the early train and which she had retrieved from the rail station in a two wheeled hand-cart.*

The stall was intended to be temporary, to last only until a permanent place could be found. It was heated, at least at floor level, by a small brazier, though Mademoiselle Saint-Eustace (the woman called herself "Mademoiselle", despite her ten year marriage to Monsieur Castaignet) had not brought briquettes for the brazier for more than a week.

*   *   *

The laughter and exclamations from holiday passengers disgorging from the tourist bus from Paris called her back to reality. A young couple-he, nineteen or twenty; she sixteen, perhaps seventeen-passed by, their arms entwined behind their backs, their hips joined while they marched in lockstep toward the quay. His face was fixed upon hers as intently as a scientist studying a specimen through a microscope, constant, unobserving of an approaching woman hidden behind an open umbrella. When they collided, brief exchanges were made, but not once did he remove his eyes from his beloved he would soon possess.

From time-to-time he flashed a smile and leaned close, very close and murmured something for her ears alone. They both exploded with laughter. Such murmurings had once entranced Louise herself, long, long ago, before all the betrayals.

Louise remembered walking along the same seawall with her parents and later, strolling with her first love, so many years before. She was sixteen, he eighteen-at that age, a world of difference.

*   *   *

"If my parents allow it, I will come to Saint-Maurice and live with you."

He shifted his weight from her and propped himself up on his elbows. He gazed into her eyes.

"You shouldn't give up school."

The sunlight through the pine branches struck her face as she looked up at him. She grasped his head and pulled his mouth to hers. They lingered over the kiss.

"There is a lady with a flower stand. I could apply with her and-" Footfalls *coming up the seacoast path alarmed them both. They sprang up, he pulling at his trouser buttons and she rearranging her dress, brushing off pine needles. They stood in mock nonchalance, facing the sea while a mother and two children passed by.*

Presently, they turned and walked hand-in-hand down the pathway along the sea toward Roscoff.

*   *   *

The tender images dissolved as she recalled the harsh letter from the youth's parents. Another romance followed at seventeen and two at eighteen and, then, the years kaleidoscopically cascading through episodes of joy, pain, alienation and, suddenly, the slamming reality of old age. The rest of the world had spun thousands of times and the young beauteous creature who used to stand in the mirror before her had turned wrinkled and old, though the vagueness of when was sadly unfathomable. Most difficult was losing ones looks. As always, it was gradual: the blush of youth giving way to creases at the corner of the eyes, contrapuntal to those at the mouth, reminders of laughter and loves long passé. And one day at the mirror, admitting that time has metastasized lines that no make-up can obscure. *In a bistro, he draws near, flashing a smile of communication and sexual expectation and you think he is approaching you. Smiling extravagantly, he passes by to flirt with the girl at the next table, the girl you once were all those years ago, those years that slipped by...slipped by...slipped by, before the ravages of age appeared.* All those elusive years until, one day, when you turned a street corner and were about to collide unexpectedly with an old woman dressed exactly like you, the realization comes that she is yourself mirrored in a merchant's kiosk. Once the unfaltering march of aging commences,

31

the forever-ness of youth weaves sinew by sinew, line by line, disappointment by disappointment, betrayal by betrayal imperceptibly into the realization that the finality of death is no longer figurative and its shadow looms beyond each morning's awakening and the turning of every calendar page. Today, here at the cold seawall of *Roscoff,* these inexorable iterations marched once again through Louise Vernet's mind.

The young lovers had vanished beyond the seawall, lost to an exotic trysting they would find magically and perhaps find magic in. She turned about and walked into the narrow *rue Pascal.* Her head swiveled back and forth, searching for a familiar sign, an image or tracings of she knew not what.

Presently, *rue Pascal* narrowed to a passageway barely two meters wide, where the sun never breached and where moss luxuriated thickly over its cobblestones. On a wall, fragments of a movie poster from the *Bijou Ciné* in *Morlaix,* in strips and tatters, announced *Captain Blood avec Errol Flynn, en English, en sous-tirer* — shards from the past, the mutilating reality of war.

I've got a ticket to Le Captain Sang...my cousin takes tickets this weekend and he would let both of us in.

I don't know...I may have to work, but...

Errol Flynn, c'est tres bon-sil vows plais...plais

O K...I suppose.

When they had made their way into the back row, beneath the projection booth, he settled into the seat and crossed his legs and sank down so that his head barely allowed his eyes to view the screen. The serial came on as the cinema went dark. A rabbit chased a crow through a field of corn and was hit on the head as the crow pulled an ear of corn off with his beak and flung it at the crow with his wings.

He eased up against the back of his seat and slipped his arm about her at the same time Errol Flynn was brushing his hand against the bare shoulder of the Empire clad lady of his moment, pulling her lips to his own. Flynn settled against her in the back seat of the coach and the camera shot up into an azure sky surrounded by the lush forest foliage as Berlioz themed up to a climax.

Louise murmured in passion as he slipped his hand into her bodice and both their hands clasped around the stiffness in his crotch.

The slamming of an opening shutter stifled her revere and she continued on. Abruptly the passageway opened upon a small square. The space had changed since those days of romantic films. Then it was plain, nondescript and a place that had come into being with neither architectural intention nor distinguishing features, a place where abutting property lines becoming fictional sometime after the sixteenth century and houses with add-on rooms and sheds collided with juttings of *Breton* half-timbering until the space morphed into a village happenstance, an opportunistic patchwork of geometric ambiguity. In this place "Mademoiselle" Saint-Eustace had opportunistically put up her modest flower stall. Louise's mind darted to the interior of the now vanished hutment and the hours sitting on a high stool, waiting, waiting for customers, customers who would invariably lift a stem from one or another vase, sniff, hold the flower out at arms length, as though it were an object deserving suspicion and finally either replacing it or setting it on the small counter for purchase. The regulars flowed in her imagination now, as though real: Madame DuCharme, the maintainer of the village's only house of ill repute, dressed in silk finery, always withdrawing only the stems she would take, no philosophical inspection, always placing these in a brocaded carry; the baker's wife, Madame Rhorbach, but a single lily, white, offering the exact change in centimes, Monsieur DuClos, the village undertaker, always impeccably dressed, carefully choosing white roses or white lilies, of the latter, occasionally lavender; the pastor's wife, always in forbidding black, high-collared, lifting roses-only roses, never any other, one by one, usually five or six, placing them-reverently Louise would think-in her shoulder strap carrying basket; the Madame who tended the *boulangerie,* three blocks towards the town center, always choosing lilacs, sniffing each stem as she withdrew it from the vase, smiling as she closed her eyes and tilting her head skyward.

Now the images withdrew and in the stall's place, a large polished black marble plinth announced from a stone wall, dominating the space. Nestled within a black *faux* magnolia-leaf surround, gold-inscribed: *Died for France in the Second World War-Renaud Penze.* She drew in a deep breath and leaned forward, steadying herself with her hand on the stone. Her eyes welled up with tears. She crossed herself and drew back, then muttered bitterly,

"For him, his soul carved in stone. For me, years in prison."

She started to move away but stopped, noticing on the wall to the left of the plinth a small bronze marker bearing the inscription *Alois Castaignet, Hero of France.* She leaned close and spit on the plaque, then turned away, her steps taking her down a street leading from the square. She continued a block and rounded a corner before she was suddenly confronted by another ghost from the past. The frosted bistro window, unwashed for a decade. Perhaps longer? A faded black and gold sign, in Augsburger font, one link broken, dangled from the corner of the building:

LE BISTRO AVIGNON

The sign squeaked back and forth, swinging in the wind. She choked back tears, her pulse racing. Here is where it all began. With a mere flirtation. And, months afterward, ended with the day the *SS* had taken her away. The stench of the boxcar, the imprisonment at Dachau and the brief freedom after V.E. Day, the shaven head, the trial at *Rennes.* No defense. The blank looks of those in the courtroom, Monsieur Castaignet's self-righteous stares, his wife at his side looking through her as the sentence was read. Hatred and loathing of those who could have come to her defense but didn't; the brutality of imprisonment.

Through the café's dingy glass, she surveyed leaning towers of stacked chairs and rickety tables all askew. Her hips hurt. She shifted her weight from one to the other and leaned against the window frame. Opening her purse, she drew out a pack of cigarettes, took one and placed it between her lips. Fumbling for matches and finding a packet, she pulled one off and struck it. She drew on the lit cigarette and stared blankly into the café.

"Where was I sitting when it all began?"

*   *   *

She sat at the small bistro table, legs crossed provocatively, the smoke from her cigarette spiraling up from a small ashtray. Her eyes traveled the room, the bar facing the table-lined wall opposite. Several German officers stood at the bar, joking. Villagers in corduroy jackets, two or three at a table, leaned on their elbows, Galoises drooping from mustached lips, murmured confidences being exchanged.

In the dim light she could feel his eyes boring into her. She fixed her lipstick, peering intently into the circle of her compact mirror, focusing on him. He was close, too close, as she knew he would be. Finished, she snapped the compact shut. His closeness tensed her, as though she were in a strange town at a street intersection under a lamp light, awaiting the approach of a stranger she had not previously met and fearful that he would appear and more fearful should he not. Aware of his fixated stares, like a cat, closing upon a bird, she feigned disinterest. Standing at the table's edge, he clicked his heels and bowed, a remainder she thought, of a character out of "Naughty Marietta" or an old World War One movie; he thrust his riding crop under his arm and, in passable French, more Alsatian than Parisian, spoke.

"Mademoiselle, may I buy you a drink?"

"Get lost, you Nazi trou du cul," she replied, less than delicately.

"I'm sure that you must understand, Mademoiselle, not all of us are here because we want to be. I myself have always been a great admirer of the French culture. I … I even have a cousin who speaks French. And…and an aunt who collects Sevres porcelain!"

"You're not sure of anything, except of the shine on your jackboots and that nasty smirk on your face, so go ahead and have me shot."

"Really, I'm not like the others."

He excused himself and disappeared out the door. Moments later, he returned, proffering a small bouquet, like a schoolboy truant, supplicating before a school principal.

"A peace offering."

With a nod of her head, she signaled the empty chair opposite her. Bereted heads turned in the room as he sat. Glowered looks traveled, lips parted to emit inaudible sneers.

"I'm just being polite, Major."

"Actually, it's Kapitain."

"Whatever, Captain. As soon as the Americans get here, you're tout fini."

"That's dangerous talk. Hitler has a secret weapon waiting for those upstarts; wait and see! Let me fill your drink and I'll forget I heard you say that."

"Do you always begin an acquaintanceship by threatening, Captain?" She elucidated three hundred years of contemptuous Franco dispraise for the Germans as she enunciated his rank.

He got up and went to the bar. When he returned, he found her gone, the flowers on the floor by his vacant chair and her lipstick-smeared Galois smoldering in the ashtray.

He stood, intensely erotic, dazed, wondering at the impossibility of seeing her and overcoming the difficulties in bringing her to his own. An unrelenting craving.

*   *   *

The next morning, across from the flower stall, a man clad in the blue smock of a railroad worker sat at a bistro table pretending to read a paper. To some, he was known simply as Renaud Penze and, to others, a leader of the Maquis resistance. She was emptying boxes of fresh flowers, geraniums, tiger lilies, pansies. The early post bus from Morlaix had dropped them off that morning. She took the long-stemmed Birds of Paradise and, one by one, put them in the tin vase on the sill. Next, she crowded small pots of violets into a shallow wooden crate placed on upturned flowerpots. She was especially careful with the roses. Carmine and blood red, they were named "Assassination" for good reason: legend had circulated that a bouquet concealed an explosive device being presented to an Austrian Duke. Another carton held pansies in variegated colors, which she also put in a small crate and set on upturned pots.

She started as she straightened up. The man in the blue smock loomed above her, standing close, much too close.

"We need to talk." His tone did not encourage denial.

"Of course, Monsieur... Monsieur?" she pressed.

"No names. I mean you no harm. Indeed, the opposite. Bistro Avignon at six", he instructed.

*   *   *

Louise pushed aside the velvet blackout curtain and peered, momentarily, adjusting her eyes to the bistro's dim light. The candlelight, a stopgap against the German proclivity to shut off the power at unpredictable times, brought Vuillardian intimacy to the room. He was sitting at a small, isolated table in a corner. He got up when she approached and grasped her in a tight embrace, bussing her roughly, on both cheeks and whispering.

"Act like you know me. Smile, like you're really glad to see me."

Louise grasped his jaws in her hands, manufactured a smile and spoke intently. "I don't know what this is all about, but if you try any tricks, I'll kick you so hard in the bijoux de famille they'll hear you in Poitiers."

"Now that we understand each other, let's get to business."

35

They sat opposite. She fiddled the crucifix about her neck and twisted and wove strands of hair, eyeing her new intimate.

The owner came from the bar and hovered. "An aperitif?"

"No, thanks. Just some vin du pays, please."

"For you, Monsieur Penze?"

"I'd like a coffee, later, thanks, Rene."

As the proprietor turned away, she twisted the crucifix and stared, in a way that would deflect a Mother Superior's accusative stare.

"You have a friendship with a certain German captain?"

"Don't be stupid. He tried to pick me up last night. I'd hardly call that a friendship."

The proprietress brought a glass of wine to the table. The woman was a cousin of Renaud's, and, Louise would learn, it was not a good thing to overhear any of his conversations lest they be part of his role as "The Shrike" in the underground Maquis. He studied her face. She realized she was being analyzed for her ability to carry out a conspiratorial task. He leaned forward and spoke.

The foghorn sounded. The rain had let up and a faint sliver of jonquil sky blossomed far out on the harbor. Now, her recollections streamed as the tide sluiced white foam that began to rock the small boats to their short freedom.

"If only I hadn't gone through with it; I should never have come back. More stupidity than bravery. So this is what I get for my fucking patriotism."

*   *   *

Chapter 7

Roscoff, the Bistro Avignon, autumn, nineteen-forty-two

She tried to conceal her inner state, and, ill at ease, she toyed with the handle of her purse, setting it first on the table and then on the floor beside her and turned to drape an arm over the back of her chair.

"You don't look like the typical storm trooper, but there is something that makes you ... different from the rest of your kind. Perhaps..." She let the sentence hang, like a luscious nibble before a hound.

He leaned forward, taut as a runner at an Olympic trial start.

"Yes? Perhaps what?"

"Oh, well, it was just an idea, my dear Boche. But, because of your stupid curfew, I must go, now." She stood up and moved to the back of his chair leaning over his shoulder and bussing him on the cheek. Her breast brushed his shoulder as she withdrew.

"Auf Wiedersehn, or, more civilized, au revoir, mein schatz." Her lips curled into a patronizing smile that, behind his back, merged to a smirk.

He turned and reached out to her, beseechingly, attempting to catch her. But she twisted out of his tentative grasp and was out the door before he could get up. He returned to his drink and found, her scent fresh on his hand, — Ivoire. He brushed his hand against his face, vowing to himself that he'd not wash the hand while vestiges of her scent lingered. At her place, a match folder. He tapped the folder on the table 'and opened it. Inside, an address, 46 rue Petain. He quaffed the last of his drink and got up and left.

Again, heads swiveled.

*　　*　　*

She stroked his head as he quieted his exertions.

"Tell me, mon Klaus, have you had it better with your Munich...how do you say it,' frawlines'?"

"Froilines, until they are deflowered, then they become Fraus."

"Beside you they are amateurs."

"Are you sure they were amateurs?"

"Well, not too sure. Probably not, but they don't have the knack for it."

"After the war and when you Germans are totally victorious, perhaps ..."

"Perhaps, what?"

"Perhaps we could live together. You aren't like the other Germans."

He slid off her and rested his chin on her shoulder.

"Do you mean that?"

"I've never meant anything more, mon cher."

"There's something I want to tell you."

"If it's any of your stupid military stuff I don't want to hear about it." She turned her face away and glanced at the bedside clock.

"It's important, I mean, important for us."

"Not if it's military. I don't want to get shot as a spy. I just want to get back to my flower stand. I told Madame Saint-Eustace I was on an errand."

"Please. I want you to know."

She placed her fingers on his lips and pulled at his shoulders as he mounted her.

She strained to reach to his ear with her lips. *"Go on and on and on, forever and forever,"* she murmured. Presently, he stilled. She shot another glance at the boudoir clock.

"So, what is this little secret you are bursting to tell me, since you seem in the mood to share everything else?"

"We are pulling out."

"I thought you just did."

He didn't like the joke. *"I mean my goddamn unit. The Eighth tank battalion..."* She clapped her palms over her ears, saying, *"I told you, no military stuff"*

"Just listen. It's a Field Marshal setting up a new headquarters."

"Oh, God, no!" (Was I convincing enough?)

"Its headquarters will be at—."

Her hand moved up and covered his mouth.

"Landerneau," he blurted out as he pulled her hand away. *"Not far from here. I can still come see you."*

"That's silly. There's nothing there, not a vineyard in sight."

"Because a corps is moving there, maybe the Third and Fifteenth, both. They don't tell me everything. I'm only a Kapitan."

"Well, if it's going to happen tomorrow..."

"Not tomorrow. Three days from now."

He pushed away from her and sat on the edge of the bed. Before he headed for the bath he started to whistle "Lily Marlene." He didn't speak again until he was standing in the doorway, toweling off.

"Another thing you should know. I came across some cash, Swiss francs. Lots of it. It's in a box. I buried it in the cemetery. In the last row, at the corner of the wall. It will help us make a new start together."

A quarter of an hour later, she looked through the window as the black Maltese cross on the staff car disappeared down the misted cobblestone streets.

*   *   *

The next morning, Louise prepared the flower stall by ritually hefting down the kiosk's security boards. As she lifted down the fourth board, she heard a now familiar sound of the Occupation — a jackboot-heel grinding sand against the cobblestones of a passageway. What normally would have irritated, today alarmed. Today, she had a mission vital to the resistance, that of passing a message to a trusted courier. Her hope of quickly putting out the plants was stampeded as she glanced aside and saw the unknown corporal, giraffe-tall and proudly tricked out in one of the thousand pairs of jackboots that had stormed across the lowlands two years before. He had paused uncomfortably, near. He crossed one ankle over the other and he stared at her while poking a wheat-straw between his teeth. Louise's breath shortened. Her arms, stiffened in fear, trembled from her shoulders as she took down another board. It was not only the scar across his cheek, but his mere presence, smile aside, notwithstanding, but his mere presence that caused her to tense. A staff car approached. He turned and shot his arm up in salute, then jackbooted off. She breathed easier only when she heard the boots clomp into the distance.

Having stored all of the sideboards against a nearby wall, she hastily distributed containers of pansies on overturned pots and arranged loose plumes in a tall crockery vase. She reserved two roses: one yellow, one red. She placed the yellow stem in a tricolor-emblazoned glass vase. Then, with her back to the bistro across the passageway, she cast her eye at the still-shuttered windows lining the street. Certain she was unobserved, she reached into her bodice and extracted a small piece of paper that she wrapped around the stem of the red rose. With little care for floral finesse, she dropped the red bloom into the mouth of the vase. On this particular day, communication was more in order than artistry.

At the bistro, an elderly gentleman put down his paper. He stood up, left some coins on the table and then strolled across the square to the flower stall. He lifted various stems, putting some to his nose and drawing in the fragrance. When he could, he studied Louise's face, looking for a sign. She smiled.

"The roses are nice, today, Monsieur Castaignet."

Neither Louise nor the man noticed that the jackboots had suddenly reappeared, apparitional, from the shadows of a nearby building. The soldier kicked the toe of his boot against the cobbles as he studied the cut flowers. Then he turned to the potted plants, asking,

"*Combien, Fraulein, sind en les argent les ... stiefmütterschen,*" he clawed in poor guttural French as to the pansy prices while swaggering about, intimating that his true interest could not be expressed while they were standing up in public.

Louise told him a price and then, panicking at the thought of the passing minutes, turned to the elderly gentleman. "And, you, Monsieur?"

He tipped his fedora toward Louise and randomly continued to sniff the flowers.

"Red and yellow, when mixed together, create orange, did you know that, Mademoiselle?"

"I thought that orange was out of season, Monsieur and they don't grow on trees here."

"Only in Seville, Mademoiselle. Which color should I choose instead?"

"I would take the yellow one, Monsieur."

"Thank you, Mademoiselle. You know my wife." He reached for the red rose. He handed it to her, taking care not to dislodge the small paper wrapped around the end of the stem.

"I would hope that your company would be as nice as your flowers. Dinner in Morlaix, perhaps next week?"

"I'm sorry, Monsieur Castaignet, but it would lead to problems. Even though I am fond of you, you know."

"But I thought after last week..."

"Last week was a mistake, Monsieur Castaigne, and now you tell me of your wife, besides."

Castaignet pressed a coin into her palm. "Adieu." And he was gone.

The German soldier, too, gave her a coin. He placed his flower on the sill of the stall and took out a cigarette. He lit it and turned to Louise.

"Merci, Fraulein." He retrieved his plant and walked slowly up the passageway and out of sight, trailing cigarette smoke behind.

Louise reached for an iris stem and placed it in a glass, her gaze following his black boots as she did so.

*　　*　　*

Alois Castaignet pushed open the back door of one of Roscoff's gray block conformities — number 21, *rue du Quay*. On a plain oak drop-leaf table in the sitting room, he operated on the red rose; momentarily unwrapping a curl of paper, like a small bandage, from the stem. He scanned its penciled words. He had no time to waste.

The narrow wooden stairs to the attic bedroom had never seemed steeper. He stepped to the nearest bed frame and lifted its foot away from the wall. He toed a chamber pot, intentionally left filthy with excrement, from a wide floorboard and then got to his knees to pry the board from the ones adjoining. A radio transmitter glistened in the exposed recess between the beams.

Castaignet lifted the transmitter from its hiding place and, using the bedstead as a crutch, stood up, the device in his hands before placing it on a table by the attic's dormer window. He threw open the shutter and reached out for the end of a thin wire that stretched nearly invisibly from a tin gargoyle on the eave. He brought the loose end of the wire to the box, attached it, tested the battery wires and then bent to translate his news into taps of Morse code.

"This is the paper hanger. I want the Chef."

In due course, a response signal tapped out.

"This is the Chef. Go ahead."

"The Third and Fifteenth Panzer Corps will be moving from the vicinity of Morlaix to Landernau commencing in two days. End of transmission."

Near the gray granite walls of *Roscoff,* a radio detection truck's antenna revolved menacingly, searching for any vagrant signal. Inside, a lieutenant scratched his chin.

"That's a strong signal for such a small place. Let's see what we can find in that house, there. Number twenty-one, I think."

*   *   *

Chapter 8

Gestapo Headquarters, Quimper, Brittany, July, nineteen-forty-two

The *Louis Seize* desk regally fronted the neo-classic parquet flooring that bespoke an era long past. Behind, windows arched from floor to ceiling. Seated at the desk, he looked at the sunlight beaming across the glistening parquet floor, occasionally glancing out at the pebbled seventeenth century courtyard dominated by a sand colored, machicolated tower, pierced below by mullioned windows. He fidgeted with his pencil, tapping it on the lacquered desktop, randomly drawing on a cigarette.

August Martin (for Luther) Bernard (for the Saint) Edouard (for a distant antecedent's affection for an English King) Friedlander had been shunted from his calling as an antiques dealer in Munich when rampaging Nazis demolished thousands of Jewish owned shops that violent November *Crystal Night*. The euphemistic *Crystal Night* was, for August Friedlander, a fortuitous opportunity: fortuitous because his newly opened shop would have fallen to economic ruin in due course because of the imminent holocaustic decimation of his potential Jewish clientele; opportunistic because he had been financed in the shop by an uncle who was wounded some nineteen years before in the failed 1923 *Putsch,* in which the Nazi leadership, Adolph Hitler, Martin Bormann and Hermann Goering had failed in an inept march on the government then in power. For some, the march was fatal. For others, like his uncle, Heinrich, then drinking away a modest plumbing shop inheritance, the machine guns opened up on the marchers as well as a grand career opportunity. Heinrich, marching directly by the future Dictator, dove for cover, but not quick enough to avoid the bullet's trajectory that could have changed history. While not mortally wounded, the bullet was an economic life-saver. When the Nazi's came to power, in nineteen thirty-three, he was rewarded with a commission in the infamous *Stürm Abteilung,* (happily abbreviated by elocutionists to SA.) and a post mortem installation in the *heldenhaft* Hitlerean national shrine. Further, he was anointed with the rank of *Oberstürmzbanführer,* the equivalent of Colonel, a considerable boost from his First World War rank as Corporal, earned while guarding a railroad tunnel the entirety of the war. With such, came perks: a spacious (and confiscated) house on one of Munich's foremost locations fronting the *Englischer Garten,* an Adler sedan and driver and three servants. It also gave him access to instant restitution for his nephew's (and his own) mistakenly damaged antique shop. For Heinrich, he parlayed the combined transactions into a substantial cash settlement and finessing a Majority in the *SS* for his nephew, August.

August Martin Bernard Friedlander, Eduard being prudently excised from the family nomenclature shortly after *Crystal Night,* being a distinct minority of those in the Gestapo holding two college degrees (Göttingen, Theology, Heidelberg, Fine Arts) aided by considerable charm and good looks.

As an antiquarian, charged with inventorying and classifying fine arts in occupied countries, with further responsibilities for assigning some to shipment to Germany; his rise to the rank of Colonel was swift, and on this particular morning a jack-booted lieutenant pranced in, shutting the door behind and moving forward, flinging his right arm skyward in a near-dislocating salute, punctuated by a click of the boot heels, a maneuver sounding like a thoroughbred hooving smartly into a courtyard.

"Herr Oberst, Lieutenant Krug, reports!"

He brought his arm down smartly as Friedlander raised his right arm lethargically, letting it fall to languid repose on the of his chair arm.

"What do you have about the conduct of,"...once more he leaned forward to the file folder on the desk... "Castaignet...Alois?"

"Colonel, Sir, our radio detection unit discovered that he was sending a signal to the filthy English and they brought him in.

I personally worked on him, but he wouldn't talk, so I used the hammer a bit. Another two days and I will get him to crack, for sure!"

"We don't have two days. His transmission gave information about tomorrow's move. Bring him in and let me try my methods."

"Jawhol, Herr Oberst,"

Krug's arm shot up in another shoulder-dislocating salute and he wheeled about, went to the door, opened it and stalked out, leaving the door slightly ajar. Friedlander rested his hands on the desk and momentarily the door was again flung open. Krug shoved a frightened, cowed elderly Frenchman forward to Friedlander's desk.

"Take away the handcuffs and pull up a chair for him and leave."

Krug quickly did as he was told and departed, closing the door quietly behind.

"I understand you enjoy playing your radio Monsieur. This has caused what some believe is a serious problem. I don't like problems, Monsieur Castaignet. By the way, what is wrong with your hands?" Friedlander asked as he observed the bloodied bandages about Castaignet's fists.

"Your soldiers hit them with a hammer, Monsieur Colonel."

"I greatly regret that. I shall look into it. Please accept my apologies. We Germans are not a brutal people, you must know that. Heinrich Henne, Schiller, Wagner, as you know are the cultural leaders of the *world*. Especially Wagner. Lohengrin. You know it of course? So *lyrical*. It expresses the real German soul. By the way, do you smoke?" Friedlander had taken out a silver cigarette case, flipped it open and was pushing it forward as he spoke.

Castaignet hesitated. A mistake. He was dying for a cigarette.

"Go ahead. They are Turkish, only the best."

He reached and took one from the case and immediately the lighter flame went to the tip. He drew on the cigarette and exhaled.

"*Merci, Danke Schoen,* Monsieur Colonel"

"Again, let me say how embarrassed I am at my soldiers...well, actually they're not my soldiers; they are from a different branch. I personally think that between intelligent people like you and me no force is necessary. If we were dealing with the Russians, or, even worse, the Jews, it would be an entirely different matter. With those, you have to use force and neither are to be trusted, but as you know, the French and the Germans were the major civilizing element in Europe, going back to Charlemagne. Charlemagne was the first of the royals to offer free education. Did you know that, Herr Castaignet? By the way, have you eaten?"

"Not since your soldiers forced the tube down my throat and tried to drown me," Castaignet replied tonelessly, fixing a stare upon the Colonel and drawing on the cigarette.

Friedlander stiffened and leaned forward over the desk, aghast. His jaw locked his lips into two narrow, waxen strips.

"They *what?*" he asked, incredulously.

"The one who brought me in here. After he smashed my knuckles with the hammer, he said that since nothing was coming out of my mouth, he would see if it would work better if they put something into it. Then his soldiers took this tube and shoved it down into my throat and poured hot coffee down it. It hurt." Leaning forward, his lips curled in tight sneer, he paraphrased, "is that what your *civilized* Schiller and Heine would do, Monsieur Colonel? Perhaps he should have set my treatment to Wagnerian music. And set me afire, too? That would have been very Wagnerian, wouldn't it?"

Friedlander, take aback, leaned away in the tapestried armchair, putting his hand to his forehead, rubbing it back and forth.

"I can assure you, I will see that there will be some severe punishment. They aren't "gentlemen"; like you and me, Herr Castaignet, they are like animals and don't obey. Here, I will order some food. And wine. Would you like some wine?"

"Would it be served the same way as my coffee, Monsieur Colonel?"

Friedlander, choosing to ignore the nuanced sarcasm, did not speak but picked up the phone and ordered some food to be brought.

44

Presently a white-jacketed orderly entered with an assortment of cold cuts, cheeses, caviar and a bottle of champagne and placed it on a table nearby.

Friedlander indicated a *chaise* and table across the room.

Friedlander poured two flutes of *Moét-Chandon*, offering to converse in French as he did so, *"nos je parle en le Francais. Monsieur?"*

He smiled to himself as he watched Alois Castaignet, momentarily turning traitorous, swill down the first flute, set it down, raising his eyes expectantly at the orderly who stood by, cradling the red-banded bottle.

*   *   *

Roscoff, the dining room at 21, rue du Quay, days later

Fleur Saint-Eustace watch her husband drop three lumps of sugar into his coffee. He had always put in three lumps, although, over the years of their marriage, he had developed an invariable ritual, placing the first lump on his spoon and lowering the spoon into the coffee until the lump gradually disintegrated, like a sand castle in a tidal wash. He would then repeat the process with the second lump. Once the third lump had dissolved, and only then, he would stir the coffee — two ritual sweeps around the cup before placing the spoon on the saucer.

As Fleur watched from across the table, she observed that his ritual took longer than usual. Her husband was disguising pain. He hid his free hand in his lap. Fleur was herself in pain. She had been upset since his late return to the house two nights before. A car had pulled up outside. Its door slammed. She could hear the motor's racing off. She found him slumped against the door. She helped him as he wordlessly climbed the narrow stairs to their bed. He collapsed there, fully clothed. She undressed him and discovered his injured hand and bruises on his side. For two days, he slept solidly. He hadn't yet said a word about it. And, now, only the chiming of her grandfather's pendulum clock and his slurping down his coffee broke the silence. She held her cup with both hands, hoping her trembling wouldn't show. At last, she spoke. "I waited. The first night I didn't go to bed. At all."

He didn't respond.

"What did they do to your hand?"

"A hammer. It will be all right."

"Did you tell them anything?"

"No."

"Are you sure?"

"Well..."

"Well, *what?*" Her voice grew anxiously insistent.

"As little as possible."

"Meaning?"

"Rien que, he averred. Better send the girl, Louise, off to your cousin's."

*   *   *

Chapter 9

A field near Roscoff, that same night

Louise stopped and bent down. Something had gotten into her shoe, hurting her foot. She felt the mud covering the outside of the shoe but found the small rock and pulled it out and flung it into the moonlit field. She continued on. The field was unfamiliar but she remembered having crossed it once years before with her family to picnic under a cluster of trees, along the shore. There would be the road up ahead, she thought and there she could get a ride to *Berven* or, perhaps *Saint Thégonnec,* beyond. Her suitcase, already heavier than she believed it would be when she had hurriedly packed her belongings. Now she stepped into a hole, ankle deep, the handle broke and it dropped into the mud. Despairing, she put it under her arm and pulled her foot out of the mud. She would not realize until later that she had left her shoe mired in the muck. A time later and tiring more step-by-step, meter-by-meter, she reached the road and stood, looking about, not knowing her way.

She was still struggling with the suddenness of her forced departure, when, earlier that night, Madame Saint-Eustace had arrived at the small house on the edge of *Roscoff* where she was renting a room, and told her that there was danger of an arrest and that she must leave quickly for her own safety. Madame Saint-Eustace pressed fifty francs into her hand and an address in *Fegreac*, a town more than one hundred fifty kilometers distant, where she said her cousin, her name written on a piece of paper, would take her in.

She stood, perplexed, reckoning space, time, helplessness, fatigue, each segment enough to drive her distraught. It was now shortly after mid-night and the fog was rolling in from the shoreline a half kilometer away. Ahead, she saw a dim light. She reckoned it would be the bell tower of the church in *Berven* and, thankful that she had at least some sense of where she was going-a town she had not heard of before, much less seen-she started trekking along toward the light. The loss of one shoe in the mud caused poor balance; she hobbled awkwardly. After a few meters she stopped and took off the other shoe.

Once more at a slow walk, her hopes arose after she saw the lights of a car from behind her. Surely the driver would stop and her hopes rose anew as she heard the motor idle down to a slower speed. She turned to face it but as the car came close, it regained speed, disappearing into the dark.

She continued on, her feet feeling the cold of the pavement, occasionally being stabbed with pain from a random piece of gravel.

She walked on, leaning against a sharp breeze that had arisen from the east, wondering how long it would take her to reach the church at *Berven*, it's distant light sporadically disappearing as a hillock or cluster of trees obscured it from view. Exactly what she would do in *Berven* was not her immediate concern; which was to get out of the muddy field. Even though she knew no one in *Berven*, she worried that if there was a danger of an arrest-Madame Saint-Eustace had not been specific-she would find a barn and rest for now she was very tired; it had been six hours since Madame Saint-Eustace had arrived at her door but now, from behind her, the lights from another vehicle, surely...

*　　*　　*

Louise dozed, her head rested against the truck's passenger seat window, oblivious to the loudness of the old vehicle's motor and the heat from the engine.

She stirred and came alert. The odor of his tobacco stench comforted her rather then repelled, because she felt safe. The driver, a Burgundian of about sixty years of age had indeed slowed and offered her a ride, not merely to *Berven* but to *Redon,* but three kilometers from her final destination of *Fegreac,* itself, where she had been directed.

"Do you always go shoeless along these roads? Mademoiselle?" the man had asked pleasantly shortly after they were once under way.

"I lost my shoe in the field. I..." Louise paused, contriving a lie to explain her presence in that particular road in that particular state of dishevelment- "had choir practice and was taking a short cut afterwards and I missed the bus to my sister's funeral and it was the only way I could get there to take care of the nephews. I was hoping to catch the train at *Saint Thégnnec,* but then you came along, Monsieur...Monsieur..." she fetched for his name.

"Montagne, Montagne, as in the Alps, mademoiselle", he replied, as he had humorously for decades, always eliciting a chuckle from the occasional listener. "And your name, Mademoiselle, if I may be so bold?"

"Louise. Louise Ver-non, monsieur", she quickly reconfigured the last part of her name, still uncertain of the dangers that lay ahead of her and of how she could trust a total stranger, no matter how friendly his mien.

Hours later Montagne's truck pulled up to the *Redon* town square, a circular fountain with a statue of Joanne of Arc squirting water into an eighteen meter concrete surround.

The dawn had broken an hour before, just as the truck was pulling into the town square. She had glimpsed her mascara scared visage in the truck's rear view mirror but she took bare notice of it, concerned about how she was to negotiate the last part of her unknown journey to an unknown place to meet unknown persons. She worried that Monsieur Renauld Penze had not spoken to her for some time and that her paramour, Captain Klaus Berwald would cause some sort of disturbance at not meeting her. He, too had been uncommunicative the past weeks. This caused her puzzlement.

She turned towards Montagne and said, "I'll wait here for my cousin. Thank you for your kindness, Monsieur Montagne. I wish you a *bon journey*."

She stepped down from the truck, her broken handled suitcase under her arm, and her muddy shoe in hand. She smiled as the truck pulled away.

*   *   *

Fegreac, the Bistro Riviera, October, nineteen-forty-two, a morning

"The beer did not arrive until a few minutes ago and as soon as I finish sweeping up, I will cool it, Madame Frouchard. Will there be any other instructions?"

"No. You are very good at what you do, Louise. How fortunate you turned up on my door step just after the *Boche* took my nephew away. He was doing everything my husband used to do and I might add somewhat better. Alois liked his cognac and after three he was simply pitiful."

"It was luck that I found your place after that horrid night I spent wandering through fields and roads. I was famished, and lucky to get a ride to *Redon*."

"My cousin phoned and warned me that you would be here, hopefully soon. I haven't seen her since a family reunion in ten...no twelve years ago. Long before the *Boche* showed up. Lord knows how long they will be here. In our area they very seldom are seen. Not enough girls, I suppose, and a town this size has very little to offer. No cinema, no park, not even a carousel. I, myself, would settle for a ride on a trained goat! She told me of the bastards that took her husband in for questioning. He was lucky they returned him to his home. I've never been there. Having a bar is a full time job. The people expect you to be open all the time and with a small family like ours, it gives us little time off, mostly on Sundays, after mass. Fortunately the *Boche* aren't around too much. Did you know that they have set up an interment camp just down the road, in a field? Lots of famous people have been taken away from Paris. Mostly Jews. Even some movie people like Jean Renoir and Rene Clair have left for Hollywood. Even some are collaborating with the Germans, Edith Piaf went to sing for our prisoners in Germany, of all places! I suppose she thought it was alright but I don't see how anyone can do that, but again when someone is holding a gun to your head, what will you do, eh?"

"If I may ask, what did your nephew do to attract their attention Madame Froucharge?"

"Someone said they saw him writing stuff on one of their posters. Like devil's horns on Hitler's photo. I don't doubt it. He was always getting into trouble at school and there was one time he got a girl at school pregnant but her parents made her get rid of it, so that wasn't hanging over our heads."

*   *   *

"That will be twenty *sous,* monsieur," Louise smiled as she set the stein of beer in front of the evening customer at the *Bistro Riviera,* Louise's place of endeavor for the previous two months, since arriving at *Fegreac.* Her low cut dress and *faux* innocent smile had miraculously increased the bar's patronage, to the great pleasure of her benefactor, Madame Froucharge, as well as increasing the number of wives who had startlingly begun to accompany their middle-aged husbands when word had been passed-quickly, too, as customs in small towns were wont to occasion-were lingering much longer, clustered around the new serving girl, laughing, cajoling, suggesting. It was the latter, the suggesting that is, such as "a walk next Sunday in the countryside?" "A coffee in the next town, even a wine and..." Sometimes more, the "more" exciting the interest of the previously home-bound spouses who in a short period of time had caused a generation of spousal frocks and dresses, hung for months unworn, to be yanked off hangers and makeup, not applied perhaps in weeks, all to be brought, with arms firmly, (definitely that), to sit at the bar, formerly only for standees, where the spouses could enjoy a society not experienced in recent times, if ever, in *Fegreac.* Even the mayor's wife, Madame Constance could examine first hand the "innocence" a frequently and unknowingly misapplied term to describe Louise Vernet's "personality" (certainly nothing more.)

It was on one of these nights, a Friday that the wind-up Victrola was being attended by Madame Froucharge, *"La Dame Au Piano"*, sung by Charles Trennet, when the bistro's laughter suddenly subsided. The patrons looked toward the door where two German soldiers both tall and bespoke poster boys for the "Strength Through Joy"[*] movement had just entered. Surveying the room, they removed their caps and placed them under their shoulder bands and stalked toward the bar. The music stopped; nervous talk resumed, subdued. Very much so.

*   *   *

---

[*] A Germanic idealization of the Nazi era, extolling the virtues of Arian perfection.

49

Fegreac, the Bistro Riviera, one week later

Louise started as she straightened up from kneeling at scrubbing the stone entrance to the door. She had not heard his foot steps.

Again, the scar on his face and the leering smile.

"Twsei Stiefinutterchen fraulein, eh?" he attempted to humorously order pansies from Louise whom he recognized as the flower seller at *Roscoff,* weeks before.

Louise attempted a smile as she got up and smoothed her skirt and stepped back into the recess of the door.

By hand signals the soldier indicated he wished to enter, with his companion, a shorter soldier, perhaps ten years younger.

Louise went in and held the door open for the two who went to a table and sat.

"Tswei caffe noir', the scar-faced one ordered in approximate French and Louise turned away, going to the coffee machine behind the bar. Two more soldiers entered followed by a farmer and his wife and a young man whose collar was pulled up around his neck. The farmer couple sat by the plate glass window fronting the street until they noticed the two German soldiers, whereupon they got up and went toward the back of the bistro and re-seated themselves with their backs to the front of the bistro. The young man also chose a table at the back and sat and lit up a *Galois.*

Louise finished taking the farm couple's order and was heading toward the bar as another couple entered and took seats near the Germans. The lady was of heavy girth and had a puffy face and heaved a sigh a she took off her coat and hung it along with her handbag over the fourth chair at the table.

Louise went to the table and took their order for a carafe of wine and a *baguette.*

As she turned away, the noted that the young man with the upturned collar was no longer to be seen. His *Galois* burned in the ashtray, unattended.

Two hours later the room had all but emptied

Of the patrons, save for the scar faced soldier, elbows on table engaged in *socco-voco* conversation with his companion.

"Now I remember when I saw her before in *Roscoff* I thought she might be lonely, I mean, *really lonely* for..." his face went into a leer and his fist emulated a sexual activity about his crotch, "but she was perhaps...tempting me...don't you think? I mean *fräuleines* do that all the time in Germany when they really, really, really *want* a guy, *nein?"*

The wine had been working its way into his brain where no doubt hidden fantasies were having a barn dance of a time pushing him towards unpredictable activities. His companion nodded in ascent as he continued. He turned toward the bar where Louise was attending to cleanup.

"Stiefmütterschein mademoiselle, *stiefmütterschen* mademoiselle, *komme!"* he ordered Louise.

Louise, her bar towel over her arm came toward the two.

"Yes, soldier? We are about to close. Something else?"

"I was thinking about when I first saw you in *Roscoff.* You were the prettiest thing I had seen ever and I was wondering..."

"Your wondering mustn't get the better of you, Sir. May I bring you another wine before we close?" she spoke, half turning away from him and smiling as she walked back toward the bar.

"*Ja. Jawhol.*" His head sank to his folded arms on the table.

"I guess she told you something, *dummkoph,* didn't she?" his companion murmured with a sneer. The Scar Face began to snore.

*   *   *

The bistro Rivera, a late evening, three weeks later

Louise had finished cleaning the tables, small and square and scarred from ringed fingers thrusting down n arguments and nicks from silverware falling astray and was writing a letter...

My dear Penze,

It's been some weeks since I have heard from...

She wrote no more as Madame Froucharge's nephew, whom she learned was the young man who had entered some weeks before, came from the back room and to her table and pulled up a chair, and sat, familiarly, folding his hands on the table in front of him.

"Claude? How surprising!"

"A wine?"

"Certainly," she answered.

"I'll fetch."

So saying, he got up and moments later returned with a carafe of red wine and two glasses.

"My aunt said you had a narrow escape from *Roscoff.* The *Boche* seem to be all around, don't they?"

"I hadn't been keeping track," Louise answered cautiously. "Your uncle got me into a bit of a pickle, with his big mouth, I believe, now that I come to think of it. He had been held for a week by the *Boche,* then they dumped him at his front door and that night your aunt came to my place and said I had to leave. He must have said something about me to the *Boche.*"

"I might be able to find out something. I'm being sent to carry some messages they don't dare send by post, everything is checked by the *Boche,* you know."

"Where will you go?"

"*Quimper,* then *Morlaix,* then to *Roscoff.*"

"Marvelous. I have a...friend. Can you carry a letter?"

"Why not? It's not dangerous is it, the letter, I mean?"

"*Mais non.* Only personal stuff. He's a good friend and I haven't heard from him.

I'm worried. It'll be a big help. I'll give it to you before you leave."

"Let me pour you another wine."

He reached for the carafe and poured and the two sat and drank in silence.

The next morning when Louise was preparing to open the bistro, she found an envelope lying on the bar. She opened it and recognized the handwriting.

"I shall return. Trust me. Claude"

*   *   *

SS Headquarters, Quimper, Brittany, two days later

SS Colonel Friedlander leaned over his desk, eyeing the young man.

"You made good time, Claude."

"I had help. One of your trucks came along and I didn't have to take the train. Some one might have recognized me, sir."

"That wouldn't do, now would it Claude? After all this is over and we are victorious, I'll see to you it get a good job in Berlin. How would you like that?"

"It would be a good change, sir. So what should I do with the letter she gave me? It does not contain anything of interest."

"Deliver it in *Roscoff.* We'll see to it that you get there. And Back. For sure. No tricks now. You were lucky we let you off easy for that clownish behavior. You can be of more value with your neighbors as our eyes and ears, as long as you keep them open and your mouth shut. Do you understand?"

"Of course, Colonel."

"You can go now. A car is waiting. Be careful, and find out what you can about that incident on the road, eh? Berwald was one of our best officers. We'll see to it that that bitch Vernet doesn't get away either."

Claude Froucharge left the room and left the chateau and entered a Maltese cross marked sedan that sped off in the morning mist.

Two days later in Fegreac, another Maltese crossed sedan pulled up to the *Bistro Riviera* and two soldiers exited. The scar-faced one instructed,

"Wait here. I want the bitch for myself."

A half hour later he returned with a bedraggled, half conscious Louise Vernet and threw her into the car and the car sped off.

Chapter 10

Roscoff, the Bistro Avignon, an evening some years after the Second World War

Decades of mélanged workingmen's sweat, cigarette smoke, and *vin-du-pays* soaked into the bistro's gouged and blistered hide walls, remaindered from the Great War, defining the aromatic ambiance of *le Bistro Avignon*. An *Empire* vintage, pressed-tin ceiling dangled green enameled shades from black, frayed-tip tentacles, reflecting the jaundiced light of five-watt bulbs onto red-and-white checkered tablecloths below. They sat, *Roscoff's* business and civic leaders, in a relaxed congeniality brewed from ancient intimacies. A wine carafe, half-empty, dominated a quartet of smudged glasses. The men, haloed by *Galois* smoke, appeared fetched from a Daumier sketch. Rene L'Estange, who supervised street repairs while his wife tended a porcelain shop near the quay, was also the leader of the town council. At 160 kilos and slightly taller than most *Roscoff* doorways, he was a man one listened to, even when he wasn't speaking. Monsieur L'Estange had recently put forth a proposal that a monument to the memory of two of the town's heroes of the Second World War be erected somewhere in the village. The purpose of the evening's gathering was to choose where and by what means. Monsieur L'Estange looked expectantly at Monsieur Duros, sitting opposite. Monsieur Duros was the village undertaker whose signature funeral processions featured a black-lacquered horse-drawn hearse (one or two horses, as the importance, or the pocketbook, of the recently deceased occasioned). The hearse was embellished with golden *fluer de lis,* an oblong glass window was engraved with frosted glass lilies, allowing a shadowy view of the deceased's casket. Duros provided cemetery monuments and, occasionally, impromptu death certificates. Encountered on the street, he would inevitably reply to the question of how business was going with a terse, "Dying." Local legend had it that one's last conversation with Monsieur Duros might be decidedly one-sided. He was also Monsieur L'Estange's brother-in-law.

Tonight, he had much to say, but tactfully would demure.

Monsieur L'Estange turned next to Monsieur "Tippey" Lavesoir, the town's barber and hairstylist and recipient of many local secrets, some of which he kept to himself.

"There is that property by the *rue Lepic,* the flower stall, that isn't of any use; why not there?"

"The one that whore — what's-her-name — Louise, worked?"

"That's the one. Madame Saint-Eustace owned it."

"Who owns it now? It doesn't seem to be open."

"It isn't. It's vacant. Someone should tear it down".

The fourth gentleman at the table, Monsieur Laval, twisted a half-drained glass of *vin du Pays* and stared, his *Galois* dangling forty-five degrees from his lower lip. He cleared his throat and was about to speak when the patron's wife glided up to the table, smiling expectantly.

They ordered a ham *baguette* for each and another liter of *vin du pais* to share. Laval cleared his throat once again and cautiously began to reveal his news.

"I was at *Morlaix* yesterday for a meeting about some new equipment."

His job as supervisor for the railroad required the wearing of a uniform that, many said, he had slept and showered in for thirty years with each decade denoted by a gold star on the cuff of his left sleeve.

"They're designing stuff that goes 210 kilometers an hour. They had pictures. Slides and all that. A regional director came out from *Paris.* He was killing two birds with one stone."

The new revelations caused the others to fall silent in astonishment. Finally, one broke their individual contemplations.

"What birds?"

"Well, first, he wanted to tell us about how the new trains will run all over France, would you believe? Three and a half hours to *Morlaix,* on special track. Eventually, two and one-half hours from *Strasbourg* to Paris *Gare Est.* An engine on each end, so they can cut out the crap about waiting for the train to arrive, then hooking a new engine onto the end and pulling it out into the yard and so on."

He took a long sip from his glass and continued. "The other thing was that he was there to supervise the unloading of a new monument for the war. They showed pictures of it. Twelve meters high. It will be just opposite the station, on that square where the bombed-out buildings were."

"We should have one here, in *Roscoff. Merde!* Those *outils* can't play soccer better than we, and they shouldn't have a fucking monument before *we* do!"

"Absolutely not!" agreed the other three, hoisting their drinks. Their drained glasses slammed onto the checkered tablecloth in unison.

And so it was decided that when *Fleurs Saint-Eustace* was demolished, an eighteen-meter plinth would replace it — six meters taller than the one in *Morlaix.*

The last carafe empty, the conversation died and the foursome arose and left.

As they walked out into the midnight air, Monsieur Duros trailed behind, smiling gleefully. He had provided the monument in *Morlaix,* specifically suggesting a size somewhat smaller than what he predicted would be the maximum height agreed to in *Roscoff.* And not only would he supply the black marble plinth with a gilded wreath surround dedicated to Renaud Penze, he would also provide a small plaque in memory of Monsieur Castaignet.

The other three paused at a corner and shook hands before heading their separate ways. Suddenly, Lavesoir turned and shouted to the neighborhood, "Vernet! Vernet! That's the name of the Boche's girlfriend!"

*   *   *

Chapter 11

Concentration Camp Dachau, Germany, fall, nineteen-forty-three

"These ten must go at the top of your list. You will have them ready in three days." The prisoner stood by the work table, enervated, emaciated, trembling, but momentarily, alive.

"Jawhol, Herr Oberst."

"Sit. And if you do well, you will get something extra."

Ishmael Tropengarten having not seen the Colonel in the camp before, glanced around like an opossum caught in a car headlights. An *SS* Corporal stood some distance away, drawing on a newly lit cigarette, nervous at not having previously been in such close quarters with a Colonel, especially one often seen in newspapers with the highest Nazi authorities. The Colonel was reputed to shoot infraction committing soldiers first, then turn to others, saying, "See what I mean?" and stalking off.

"These must be absolutely perfect. Perfect."

He flared out the papers like playing cards on a poker table.

"Perfect."

He pointed to one small photograph, that of Heinrich Himmler, dreaded chief of the *Schutstaffel,* or *SS.*

"This one is to go with the one in the Corporal's uniform. Do not ask questions.

Do not, under any circumstances, talk with anyone about this."

He got up. Tropenhagen scrambled to his feet, grasping his beltless, shitted striped trousers with one hand, saluting with the other.

"No one."

He spun about and stomped out.

*   *   *

Concentration Camp Dachau, three days later

Tropengarten fingered the documents and whispered to Isaiah Goldschmidt seated nearby,

"These are identity documents. Not exactly like the British 20 Pound notes we have been doing, huh? Here, take a look."

He pushed the stack of papers over to Goldschmidt, who began examining the documents critically, muttering to himself.

"These are new...high ranking guys. Keitel, Bormann, Friedlander. Fried...lander. Whose he? And Himmler in a corporal's uniform. A *Corporal! Heinrich Himmler! Uncroyable!*"

Companion photos in the same file depicted revealed the same officers in various civilian attire. He shoved the pictures back to Tropengarten.

"Spies, perhaps," Tropengarten thought to himself. The pack in hand, Tropengarten examined the first one, a photo of an angular-jawed *SS Colonel* identified by the last name of Friedlander. The identity paper bore French watermarks and the passport covers were new and of French origin. Friedlander's was inscribed, *Ambrose Sonomme.*

Slurping a cup of watery soup and a hunk of stale bread, Tropengarten looked furtively about and slid over on his work bench to his fellow prisoner. He held open one of the engraved identity cards, shoving in front of Goldschmidt, asking,

"Do you like my work?"

Taking the document and placing it under his microscope, he affixed the eyepiece and studied it and slowly drew back and turned his head,

"Marvelous, Trope. How did you think of that?"

Then after a moment's hesitation, and in a loud whisper, "if they discover what you've done, they'll *kill.*"

Shuffling of feet and the slamming of the frame door quickened his passing the newly and curiously minted document back to Tropengarten. The two sprang to attention as *SS* Colonel Ringshoffer clomped towards them, commanding in an almost genial manner,

"Sit"

"Show me what you have."

Tropengarten removed the documents from a cardboard box and placed each, side by side, along the table to and waved his hand across them looking up at Ringshoffer.

Ringshoffer picked each one up and studied one after the other, muttering ingratiating complements as he did so..

"Good positioning of the official stamp...Picture transposed very well...can't tell it from the real thing...good work...excellent, ah what's your name, Jew boy?"

"14 254 3, Herr Oberst."

Ringshoffer finished his examination and put the documents into his brief-case. One for his nephew Friedlander, one for himself and one each for seven higher-ups. Turning towards the door he ordered,

"Come with me. For the reward I promised you."

Tropengarten shuffled his scant body up and toward the door being opened by an alert *SS* Corporal. Holding his filthy striped trousers up with one hand, he shuffle-hopped out and down the two steps. Ringshoffer followed behind, slowly reaching toward his pistol holder as the door closed and Isaiah cringed in fear. Two shots rang out.

*   *   *

Chapter 12

An hour later on the highway to Berchesgaden

Soon to be the late Colonel Heinrich Ringshoffer, wheeled the Adler sedan away from the central Post Office in Munich where he had just mailed his nephew, August Friedlander, his new identity document, with a letter explaining:

"Even though we will be ultimately victorious in our Germany's rightful crusade against the Jews and their allies in the west, the recent turn of events in Poland are making me nervous. Even though the Führer has plans for a new secret weapon, the damned British don't seem to want to give up and the Americans may have more power than we realize. Our navy is performing brilliantly in sinking most of their ships. Nevertheless, since our higher-ups are providing themselves with an alternative identity, just in case, -and keep this to yourself- I thought it prudent for you to have some way for you to find my dear wife, your aunt, staying in a quiet area of Paris while working for our Red Cross.

My dear nephew, *Heil Hitler!*"

He wheeled the car through the narrow streets and onto the newly constructed *autobahn* towards the Alpine enclave of Germany's highest.

The alpine splendor rose in all it's majesty on his right and he slowed as he diverted from the autobahn to a narrower, two lane highway. The sunset was striking the cliffs of one of Bavaria's postcard vignettes, a behemoth facet of one-thousand meters. Ringshoffer recalled hiking up the pathways leading around the more subtle stretches of the granite pre-history after the first war, before the *Putsch* of 'twenty-three. Now the air was the same, clear and lung stimulating. Instead of patched *lederhosen* and sleeping in a farmer's loft- (fifty-*phennings* and a glass of warm milk in the morning, shot direct from the heifer's udder by the skilled teat-pull of the farmer's wife), he, Heinrich

Ringshoffer had stayed the previous evening in a four-star lakeshore hotel in Bad Wiessee and this morning was clad in a ribbon-decorated uniform of the finest wool. He mused that his accomplishment of what he earnestly believed was a confidential task, would bring him a special reward. Little did he know, how special the reward would be, but hours from where the *Heur* watch on his wrist ticked away his last few hours on earth.

*   *   *

The sun was an orange fireball resting on a distant landscape showing in his rearview mirror as the Adler pulled up to the spiked iron gate of Germany's third ranking Nazi, Heinrich Himmler, a self-promoting former poultry farmer whose transition from killing edible feathered creatures to burning humans, seemed, to him to be but a natural progression.

Ringshoffer glanced easterly at the high promontory, the *Adlerhorst*, (Eagle's Nest) the spectacular-and intentionally intimidating residence of the Dictator, Adolph Hitler. Ringshoffer wondered if the man would be there at this very moment, looking his way; *"is he looking down at me; did he remember that day in 'twenty-three when I took a bullet for him, did he, right now, did he?"*

His momentary revere was interrupted by an SS soldier stalking up and standing by the car window. Ringshoffer rolled it down.

"Nom, bitte, Herr Oberst"

"Ringshoffer...*für der Reichsführer SS.*"

The solder sprang back and saluted smartly, and waved his arm.

The gate swung open and Ringshoffer wheeled the car to the front entrance, a bespoke wide-planked pine door; solid, hinged by spear-pointed iron hinges that signaled regal authority, the antithesis of the more modest Bavarian eves and pacific window shutters of the structure's remainder.

An SS soldier sprang from no-where and flipped the door open, and saluting, offered a standard-greeting, "Heil Hitler!"

Ringshoffer exited the car, and turned back, reaching across the driver's seat to retrieve the document-holding brief case. Turning, he plowed his Wagnerian girth toward the door and up three broad steps to the door.

Nervousness mixed with pride of accomplishment rushed through his veins. The last-and only time-he had seen the Reichsführer was at one-hundred meters distance in the Olympiad stadium in Berlin in 1936. Surely the personal contact on this day was to be significant and he felt exultant. The first definitely would signal big career move. The second, was sub-minimally warranted but was attended with a post-mortem career option, and he continued to stride strode confidentially up to the shellacked pine door.

Instantly at his approach, the door was pulled open, and an SS Lieutenant stepped smartly one pace forward, rendered an arm jolting salute,

"The *Reichsführer SS* is expecting you. Did you have a pleasant trip, Colonel?" Without waiting for an answer, he continued,

"Please follow me."

He strode with parade ground steps, mimicking leaps, for the twenty meters until the two were where another door menaced. He rapped twice and, when the customary *"herein"* muffled through the door, the officer opened the door and stood aside for Ringshoffer to go in, pulling the door shut after.

Himmler was sitting in an arm chair placed before a panoramic window, the flame ball sun by now sunken to a half-sphere revealed against a mountain profile. Ringshoffer stood at attention, and saluted. Himmler arose and with unusual geniality beckoned the hapless man forward.

"A pleasant journey, Ringshoffer? Better roads now, than back when, no?" Without waiting for a rejoinder, he continued,

"You have something for me, I trust." And he thrust out his hand for the briefcase, vigorously plunging his hand into it, seemingly searching for something other than documents, which, for a spurious revolver, he actually was. Satisfied that he would not be assassinated, he seemed to relax into a state of geniality and offered Ringshoffer a chair opposite.

"One can't match *Offenbach* for good German handmade leather, eh, Ringshoffer? Others may come close but the quality of the tanning-it's all in the horse-piss, did you know that, Ringshoffer? The world thinks that horses are only good for racing, but it's their *pissing* that really counts! And the racers are out of action by the time there are four or five, but a good old non-racer can piss his way into eternity!"

"Now, let's see what we have here"

He began examining the documents one-by-one, murmuring as he did so,

"The Führer tells me you were at the march in 'twenty-three. How intriguing. He was lucky, indeed, all Germany was fortunate that he was not wounded as you were. These...documents one for Keitel... one for me...and several others, one...for... yourself..." he looked up questionably...very thoughtful. Quite thorough. Tell me. Was this work kept very confidential, Ringshoffer?"

"Absolutely, *Herr Reichsführer.* Only the workman at Dachau, one of the best at bank notes, I might add, and *only myself.*"

"Can we be sure the workman won't talk?"

"Absolutely. I followed your instructions to the letter."

"And the workman?"

"He met with a serious accident, *Herr Reichsführer*, only moments after he handed these over." Ringshoffer shrugged and proffered a conspiratorial, knowing smirk.

"Ah, I see. Accidents *will* happen. So, you must be anxious to take a few days leave. My car will take you."

Both stood and Ringshoffer slammed his boots together and did an about-face, went to the door and shot his arm up in salute and rendered the obligatory,

"Heil Hitler, *Herr Reichsführer!*" and did another about-face and marched out the door.

Outside, his own car was nowhere to be seen. The engine of another Adler purred.

"*Reichsführer's* orders, Colonel Ringshoffer. We are to escort you."

Ringshoffer felt a strong arm of another man shove under his own propelling him towards the open door and finding himself between two leather-coated *Gepos'*, a type he recognized inferentially, having spent his early party days in such capacity. The door slammed shut and the driver, glass-partitioned from the back seat, sped out the gate.

*   *   *

A quarry, in Forest Tannenbaum, some miles distant, the same evening

Second Lieutenant Gernot Burkheiser stood over the prone *SS* private and instructed, "It won't be long now. When the car comes, wait for my signal. The lights won't come up until the car gets here. I think I'll tap you on the shoulder if you have to shoot. There may be one or two or even three. Make sure the bolt is pulled back on the machine gun; might as well do it now. The soldier obeyed, and pulled a side lever of the gun.

The crunch of boot steps through the gravel alerted them and Burkheiser stood up as his name was spoken,

"Burkheiser?"

"Ja.. wer ist? Ach, Captain Kanzler. It's dark and..."

"Yes, I know. Now, here's an important message from headquarters. It is to shoot *all* in the car, no questions. It is high level security and it never happened, do you understand?"

"Yes, Herr Captain. All in the car. I understand."

"I will flash a light as a signal. And after it is over, the bodies go into the pool, understand?"

"Yes, Herr Captain, understood, completely."

"They are all traitors, so don't let your conscience bother you. You may be rewarded, by the Führer, himself."

*   *   *

"I appreciate the escort, gentlemen," Ringshoffer proffered with polite uneasiness, "but I only have to go to the rail station for the sleeper to Berlin."

Neither *Gepo* responded and the one on Ringshoffers right leaned forward and out of the back seat pulled down a tray and folded his arms. The car sped into the dark, the back seat passengers remaining silent. After and hour, the sedan slowed and turned into a field, beyond which it sped into a pine-timbered forest. A kilometer, further, it pulled into a clearing, stopping shortly before a granite cliff-surrounded lake. The larger of the *Gepos* pulled out a pharmacy packet from his coat pocket and took out a capsule.

---

*   Euphuism for Gestapo Nazi security force, separate from the SS, SA

Instantly, the quarry came ablaze with floodlights. Outside, Ringshoffer saw that the car was surrounded by machine guns, manned by helmeted storm troopers, fingers on triggers.

Both *Gepos* exited from the car, leaving Ringshoffer in the back seat, sobbing and terrified at the prospect he knew was ahead, having himself engineered several escapades such as this in the early 'thirties when Adolph Hitler was "running for office." The *Gepo* at the right door lowered his head through the door and spoke deliberately,

"Either take the pill and receive a state funeral at the *Heldenhalle* or," he waved his arms toward the guns, "your family will never know what happened to you." So saying, he stepped away and was caught by a hail of bullets fired from both sides of the car. His companion *Gepo* on the opposite side of the car broke into a run toward the forest and was clipped ten meters away, falling face down in the gravel, his legs jerking for the last few seconds of his life.

SS Captain Rudolph Kanzler stalked toward the sedan, his pistol drawn, unaware that Ringshoffer, having quickly assessed the action, had drawn out his own pistol concealed under his tunic. Kanzler had just yanked open the door when Ringshoffer's bullet cut into his forehead.

As Ringshoffer collapsed, Lieutenant Burkheiser, his machine gun lifted from the tripod advanced toward the car, the door flung open and Ringshoffer plunged out, swearing profusely but incompletely as his nephew Burkhesier's stream of bullets cut him short, lurching him into the quarry pond.

The lights still glared but the place fell quiet, save for the sound of boots crunching about in the gravel.

The moon vanished behind the clouds as the assassination squad gathered the remains of the *Gepos* and pitched them into the quarry. Then, silently they climbed aboard a truck and waited for Lieutenant Burkheiser who was glancing into the recently assaulted car. He reached in took up the late Colonel's hat and carried it to the truck and leaped on. The truck headed through the darkened forest back to the nearby barracks.

The next morning Burkheiser would discover the name inside of the murdered Colonel's hat: August Ringshoffer, his uncle.

*   *   *

Chapter 13

A country road near La Trinité-Porhoét, Normandy, September, nineteen-forty-four

He shifted about in the hard seat-there was no cushion-and glanced down at the stone pinion marker on the side of the road: *Trinité-Porhoét 61Km*, the indented letters but faintly visible after decades of weathering. The marker was shaped mordantly like a grave-stone, installed nationwide by a government-coalescing tire manufacturer in the `twenties.

He was tired. He accustomed to being driven about in a sedan and not used to driving a truck, much less all night long over rutted country roads. The hours previous to his undertaking were spent in painting over the German Army markings, one of which, the "double lightning" insignia of the dreaded German *Schützstaffel,* would have made the truck decidedly unpopular in the countryside, much more so at number *6 rue Taclet* in the twentieth *arrondissement* of Paris, his intended destination, the home of his aunt, Madame Francene Duclos, with whose late husband Heinrich, he shared ownership of an antique shop in Munich, those many-so it now seemed-years ago, when *Siege Heils!* rang out with manic frequency throughout the Third Reich. And when the Master race, then wildly optimistic about the certain victory ahead, swarmed into Austria without a shot; Czechoslovakia the same but then came those fractious Poles and the final affront to the Master idyll, those obstinate French, most of whom slunk away as the first *Panzers* rumbled around the "impregnable" Maginot line, led from suburbia in England by the totally obdurate, Charles DeGaulle. For the most part the French "cooperated" when confronted with *Schutzstaffel* reasoning, only a few choosing unwisely to blow up trains, (some of them, even their own.)

Now, all the *Sieg Heils* had been muted by the realities of defeat. Friedlander, two years prior, had been told of his uncle's mysterious death.

Now, on this hot August day in nineteen forty-four, the throbbing of the engine, worn from too many conquests along rutted roads, was laboring. The nightlong drive had numbed him. Episodes from the past sliced into his mind, mingled with the blurred vision of the day's long drive. He had tricked out the truck with the French tri-color on the rear bumper and muddied it over to disguise the less than twenty-four hour old paint. His distant memories and the reflected glory of his uniform and black-polished boots demurred to concern at the approach to the river *Yvel*, with the predictable guard post and more rivers and guard posts threatening, beyond. Now in the shade of a roadside copse he would wait for dusk, before continuing on. He pulled the truck to the side of the road and drifted off, *Sieg Heils!* of the past mingling with strains of *Horst Wessel Lied,* and dreams of his first assignments in the *SS* the grandeur of the French museums, soon to be denuded of their treasures; the boring assignment of the roundup of the Jews at *Drancy,* culminating in the intelligence command at *Quimper,* residing in Breton regal splendor, spreading his talents between ferreting out thankless French free fighters and dispatching priceless antiquities to the safety of the Third Reich.

*   *   *

Friedlander awoke and started the truck and eased it toward the guard shack—a telephone booth-sized, tar-papered structure and stopped. Reaching over to the passenger seat, he took up a brown wallet with imposing papers identifying himself as one Ambrose Sonomme, residing at number *6 rue Taclet,* Paris. He sat, waiting for the guard, propped against the structure, to arouse himself. Moments passed. He gazed about. The guard blissfully slept.

Friedlander tapped the horn and watched for the guard to stir awake. But he didn't, so Friedlander pressed the horn again, this time holding the button down for a longer time. He watched for a movement. None. Thinking the man had been overcome by the contents of the wine bottle lying nearby, he took the identity packet from the passenger seat and dismounted and leapt over the narrow drainage ditch and up to the slumbering soldier, his blue garrison hat pulled down to his eyebrows. At close range, Friedlander sensed it strange that the sleeping soldier's eyes were open. And so they were. But in death, unseeing. His stomach had bled burgundy ooze from a gaping wound. A bloodied bayonet lay nearby. Friedlander needed no further motivation to depart the scene quickly and he made a leaping trot back to the truck and accelerated the short distance to the river and crossed to the other side on a temporary bridge installed by the military to replace one destroyed by contentious forces. He accelerated up the red clay embankment and headed down the road. Presently, the road curved to the left to navigate the obstruction of a high bluff materializing ahead. As he steered around the curve he slammed on the brakes to avoid hitting a spread-eagled soldier, dangerously straddling the rutted road.

Before he was aware of it, the soldier, an American, was by the door,

"Bon Swear, monsewer. Carreyeze vous mose?"

65

Reacting to the fractured French, he instinctively knew to be American, partly because the soldier's khaki shirt bore a red diamond on the left shoulder, one Friedlander knew to be an American divisional ensign, Friedlander pointed to the passenger side and the soldier ran and pulled the door open and leaped into the seat.

"German truck, huh?" he turned his head and smilingly questioned.

"It was, soldier, but now, I'm proud to say those lousy Germans left it behind and it belongs to France!" Friedlander replied, affecting a French accent.

"My name's Billy Joe Ramaker, monsewer. Which way are you going, monsewer?"

His voice was comatose, nasally, definitively American.

"To Paris I must bring this load of furniture to a shop. I have special permission from the government because they want to get commerce alive again. And you?"

"I have to catch up to my unit so I guess Paris is where I can do that. I got off my truck to get some cigs in a shop and they took off without me. I hope I'm not in trouble. So now that those fuckin' Krauts are gone, will there be a lot of checkpoints do you think, monsewer?"

"I suppose." He shifted down as the truck came up against a deep rut.

"Wouldn't you make better time if you got this piece of shit onto a paved road, monsewer? Of course it's none of my business, I mean I'm glad for the ride and all but this is taking us fuckin' forever. Excuse my French." He chuckled at his joke.

Friedlander explained as he continued to steer,

"The paved roads are still clogged with people who went to *Bordeaux* during the first part of the war. Petrol is short and when they run to empty, they don't always get the car off the road and it has to be pushed and it holds everything up."

At *Shablie,* three villagers sat on a bench in a small park as a church bell chimed, a calico cat, half-starved, slunk warily along the road and four hours later, *Vendome.* Ramaker continued to nasal on,

"Back home we have a lot of wagons that slow things up, especially on Saturdays when everyone is going to market. You get behind one of those fuckers and you go ten miles an hour if you can't pass, because of the hills. My old man has a 'twenty-nine Essex and it can goose along up to sixty, flat-out. He had a 'thirty-three Chevy but it was a piece of shit and his uncle died, so he got the Essex. The interior was shot but it drove neat, had the thermometer sticking up out of the radiator up front. Dad painted it a bright orange. Could see that sucker comin' from miles away."

He nattered on. *Casse de Vivien* and another river, *Brayenmore-Querlaime, Villes Charlenague,* forested copses articulated around fields, yellow with uncut wheat. A four way intersection and a sharp left turn and twenty kilometers to *Saint Loup du Dord.* Vacant cobbled streets, red tiled roofs with gaping holes, tattered curtains flapping out of broken windows, shutters askew, hanging on by a hinge, a bloated dead horse, legs straightened in death's paralysis, it's overturned wagon spewing Boche ammunition, a mordant reprise of the month's carnage just passed.

The soldier continued a monologue almost non-stop until Friedlander noticed thankfully-that he had quietly fallen asleep, his head resting on the door frame. They passed through *Saint-Poix Evron:* shops closed, shutters drawn over dormered windows, a stray cat, thin, emaciated, slinking across the dirt street to the shade of a wall; a town deserted, fetched from a macabre play.

Once through the village, open mustard fields, then in monotonous slow order, more villages and to *Saint-Amoult-en-Yvel:* another river to cross. Friedlander looked over at the soldier, sandy-haired and unshaven. Glancing down, he noticed the soldier's bayonet scabbard.

Empty.

*   *   *

The truck dogged along, time dragging with it, the dirt road relieved only by an occasional fording of a stream diverting a blown bridge. Irregular, forced slowing by deep ruts and occasional dead horse, bloated from days of heat, which were now becoming almost unbearable. Then the sun went down and they drove through the night and into the dawn and another hot afternoon. The soldier dozed and, from time-to-time suddenly awoke with an obscene shout, followed by groping for a cigarette, then lighting it and falling asleep once more, the lit cigarette dangling from his lips. Finally he awoke, and straightened up.

"Have you been to Paris yourself, monsewer?" the sandy-haired American asked in the same nasally grinding voice that Friedlander disliked from the first time he heard it, the day before. Ambrose Sonomme, Friedlander's new identity, was sweating in Isaiah Goldschmidt's *Breton* corduroys. Presently they exchanged places, with Ramaker driving which he had offered to do because Friedlander was tired and at this point really didn't care. Ramaker was a truck driver in the United States Army before he "was left behind," as he had put it.

The American flicked the ash off his cigarette out the window and held its half-remains at the top of the steering wheel. He continued to draw on the cigarette until he finally flicked it out of the window and reached for another from the pack of Camels on the dashboard. Friedlander's discomfort grew as his eyes periodically shifted towards the empty bayonet scabbard.

"Do they have any cheap hotels? I mean the army may be slow with my mustering out pay and I might have to find work, I mean before they ship me home." As he spoke he drew out a wad of money from his pant pocket and proceeded to thumb through it. Friedlander glanced over. The bills were in French francs, large, beautifully engraved. And in large denominations.

His mind swirled with anxiety. He knew that the Americans paid in small bills called "script", having the appearance of a game-board accessory. His anxiety grew as he became suspicious of Billy Joe's source of so many francs.

Before he could frame more thoughts, they were approaching a check point a hundred meters ahead. Billy Joe tensed and pulled at Friedlander's sleeve.

"Hey, monsewer, I've got to take a leak. Howabout you stop this rig and let me take care of that; then I think I'll get in back and grab some shut-eye in one of them there couches in back, huh?"

He was out the door before Friedlander could reply.

Friedlander got back into the driver's seat and began pulling the truck to a full stop at the check-point. He heard foot-falls behind and the back tailgate cover being brushed aside and Billy Joe thumping aboard. He came to a full stop as he reached the checkpoint. An American Military Policeman signaled to halt. He held out his new identity card as the soldier came up to the side of the truck, white block-lettering "M. P." on the black arm-band emblazoning his authority.

"Bong Swore, monsewer. Avez vous les papers?" The soldier asked in mangled bespoke Franglaise.

"Of course, here they are," Friedlander answered in English. "I'm a furniture dealer returning from Normandy."

"I'd like to see what's in the truck, monsewer."

"Of course. But the back tailgate doesn't work well. You can see what you want from the passenger seat."

The soldier went around to the passenger side and opened the door and stood leaning over the seat-back and peered into the darkened recesses. As he turned back to Friedlander he noticed the pack of Camels on the dash board.

"You smoke Camels, monsewer? I thought all you Frenchies smoked them blue ones, Gal something-or-other?"

"*Galois*, Lieutenant."

"Corporal, but thanks for the promotion."

"My passenger bought them in a shop in Tours...he said," Friedlander gave a questioning roll of his eyes as he passed a warning.

The soldier's genial smile faded as he picked up the Camels and murmured, "These have an army 'duty-free' seal on them; they aren't for...sale...anywhere. Step out of the cab, monsewer."

Ambrose Sonomme did as he was told. And quickly, too. His experience in the *SS* had shown him that people slow to understand were often shot. He didn't realize that the American army was more subtle.

From the guard house a young Lieutenant—Friedlander noticed the gold bar on his helmet—advanced. The Corporal saluted.

"Sir, there's something about this guy in back I don't understand..."

*　　*　　*

Paris, rue de Belleville, two days later

Ambrose Sonomme-he was now accustomed to the name, having presented himself under varying and nervously times with his forged Dachau identity papers-slowed the cumbersome *ex-Wehrmacht* two-tonner along the *rue de Bellville*, looking for the intersection of *rue Saint Croix*. He had driven through the southern reaches of Paris in the early morning after pulling over somewhere in the countryside late night to rest. Now, suddenly, the enameled *rue Saint Croix* affixed to a building corner was almost upon him. Quickly he wheeled right and pulled the massive truck up onto the curbed sidewalk. He reached for the ignition switch, but the truck, a tired warrior of sorts, having driven victoriously along country roads in Poland and defeated routes much later in France, choked out in a despairing final gasp of defeat, weeks later to be emptied of furnishing exotica. Years later, it's rusted bed would serve ingloriously as a swine feeder in *Bordeaux*. Sonomme sat back and stretched over to the passenger side and looked upward for the building number. Presently, he saw it: a gold "6" pressed into forest-green coloration, distressed by coal grime, indigenous since the time of Molier and Offenbach and fallen to further neglect during the recent Occupational strife.

He sat, thinking, wondering how to present himself to his aunt, wondering, if indeed, she was still living at the address his uncle had given him after that *Kristalnacht*, twelve years-seemingly centuries-ago, a November night when he would be yanked from the tangled, enchanting milieu of Baroque gilt and doleful-eyed Vermeeresque Dutch maidens, seated, staring out from sixteenth century splendors; propelled into a cataclysmic violence that he, Friedlander, did not invent, the antithesis of his perceived purity of his 'teenage *Hitlerjügend*, memories of campfire Idylls in the Black Forest; and the Alpen Tegernsee; the running and jumping and the recitations, at all of which he excelled, not realizing to where it would all lead. And when it did so lead, the exhilaration of the uniforms, the marching, the glimpse of Hitler, not merely the radio voice, but Hitler, *himself*, real, not in a grainy news flick, standing in the open Adler limousine, arm extended in salute but meters from where, he, Wilhelm Friedlander, tall, and able to see above the others, stood, intoxicated with the infecting power. That was the day he wanted to be that man, riding in an open car with thousands cheering and *hachenkreuz* flags flapping to the beat of jackbooted stomps and militant drum-beats. That was the day that Friedlander recalled, the instant the motor died and the kaleidoscope events since, began shingling through his mind, like cards in the dealer's shuffle at a casino; first, a night sometime before at a casino with his uncle, a SS Captain, draining a beer *krug*, sharing the Munich *Kristalnacht*, still, years later, fuming in contempt,

"*Those scheisekopfs couldn't get anything straight. They were given a fucking map. They were supposed to hit the Jew place next door, the delicatessen. Those scheisekopfs can't tell a high class art shop like ours from a fucking würst shop; we'll never get back the Rhineland. At that rate we couldn't capture a rabbit hutch. I told* *them the SS should have been in charge, but oh, no, that fairy, Roehm*-he was behind me in the Putsch-had to get his two Groschen in and that's why we were squatting behind sandbags for two hours!"*

Other episodic shuffling followed: the assignment at the Reichs Conservancy in Paris, a five-star hotel accommodation at the Place de Concorde, with those surely French waiters who always took their time getting the food to the table, and the rude French diners who would suddenly stand up from their restaurant table when, any of us entered and swiftly depart, hastily flinging money onto the table and giving a grim eye to the waiter; it was hard to be amongst people with such attitude.

"Actually, we had not killed many of them; only the idiots that tried to hold us up with that "impregnable" Maginot line and they deserved to die because they were so stupid to believe that anything could stand up against the cleverness of our General Staff and our Panzers!

They actually didn't understand that it was the unfairness of the Versailles Diktat** that brought us to restore the German right. They had taken all our mines in the Rhineland and all our ships and all our rail rolling stock and it was only right that we could govern better than they. We had every right to be there. Since our arrival, the trains began running on time! And many of the young maidens were friendly with our soldiers."

The slamming of the tail-gates in the fourth *arrondissement* in July, 1942 and how grubby those Jews looked after only two or three days at *Drancy* before we shipped them off to work in the factories in the East. And all that useless stuff they brought with them!

He lit a cigarette and drew it in as he thought about the contents of his truck, a priceless collection confiscated from the finest museums in France that he had prudently put aside at *Quimper.* He looked down the roller-coastering *rue J la Croix,* in *Belleville.* His eyes traveled the small church tower, *Cour le Saage,* one square ahead and, over his right shoulder, *Place Fréhal,* ell-shaped into the corner, half-surround next to antebellum constructs, one of them the vacant shop immediately beneath his destination, number six.

He was unaware that through third floor shutter louvers at that very address, an elderly woman, Inspector Cérese Brevard, alias as Frau Gudran Ringshoffer squinted and turned to a visitor,

"I think that may be him, now."

"I'll go now. Keep me informed. Practice your German".

" Danke schoen. Pour les Francais!"

"Pour les Francais!"

*   *   *

---

*   Ernst Roehm, original compatriot of Hitler; rival of Himmler, killed in Munich during "Night of the Long Knives."

**   The German colloquialism, a truism for the Versailles Treaty.

Chapter 14

The bibelot shop on rue Saint Dominique, fall nineteen-fifty-five

She straightened up, startled at his presence. The small hunched plaster alarm cat had not "meowed" when the man entered. Tall and distinguished, with an angular, jutting jaw, wearing a fall jacket, he stood in front of the counter, smiling expectantly. She had just laid out the new *peau de soie* in the display window and chirped a friendly," 'soir", while scooping up the cat and turning on its switch. Then she darted behind the counter and beamed up at him. *"Quele que nos enchantément pour vous, Monsieur?"* she enticed, gesturing with a sweep of her hand above the glass case.

"Actually, I have a few trinkets. An aunt of mine has died and she collected things. Quite a lot, as a matter of fact. No one in our family has any interest in them so I have decided to sell." He hesitated, then, as an afterthought, continued, "and give the money to charity."

"Of course, Monsieur. Do you have the objects, Monsieur...Monsieur?" she prompted for his name.

"Sonomme...Ambrose Sonomme. I have them in the bag, here." He lifted the small satchel up to the counter, and, becoming engrossed, took out baubles, one by one: rings, bracelets, lockets, watches, necklaces, a mini-circus parade of enticement, enchantment, love, and devotion. She murmured alternately, *"Ah,"* and *"Regard,"* as he laid them on the counter-top. But soon her voice fell away as she shifted her gaze from the baubles to the man's jacket.

And the *petit-point* collar she had made more than a decade before for her brother. She continued to watch, trembling, transfixed, studying his features, the high cheekbones, today somewhat more sallow but the head tilted arrogantly upwards toward the Parisian skies; today she superimposed her yesterday's image viewed from the *Marais* attic to blend with the features of the man sorting through the belongings of many yesteryears. Minutes later he had laid the last out on the counter and looked at her and smiled. She forced a slight smile to her lips commenting, "I can see your aunt had good taste, Monsieur Sonomme; there must be a lot of history amongst these, but *non*, Monsieur?" she intoned with intended double meaning. If the subtlety penetrated, he did not show it as he looked at her, questioningly.

Her voice was calm, but inwardly she was in emotional havoc.

"My cousin makes all the decisions with me, Monsieur...Sonomme," she fabricated. I can give you a rough estimate only, certainly not binding and then give you a figure in about a week. Our terms are forty-percent commission..."

He drew away in mild abjuration. "Forty percent! Isn't that quite high? I had thought more like ten...or fifteen...Mademoiselle."

She started to pick the items up and re-wrap them as she spoke,

"That is the best we can do, Monsieur. You will find the same rates all over, so, if you wish, I will help you pack these; they are very nice indeed...and...but you must understand these are very old and styles change and some of these stay with us for months, I hope you understand and..."

She did not need to finish the sentence.

"Of course, if that is the best you can do, I've made a list and you can sign it as a receipt, Mademoiselle."

"Agreed, Monsieur."

Together they took the collection and, one by one, checked them off the list he had brought. He placed each one on the counter and she found it on the list and put a small check-mark by each, and within a half hour they were finished.

It was a tension-filled episode for Sarah Goldschmidt. She had acceded to the ownership of the shop a few years after the war when her uncle had failed to return from one of the camps to which the former *SS* Colonel August Friedlander, had consigned him. Friedlander who, on this very day and wearing the same jacket she had embroidered for her beloved brother, Sascha, had entered her shop.

As the visitor from the past went out, she thought the guard cat's wail was unusual, somehow different. As the door slammed, it was not the shop door Sarah Goldschmidt heard. It was the slamming of the Gestapo truck tailgate and it was the image of the man who had just left—below her *Marais* window, by the truck, standing in studied arrogance—that she recalled. She put her elbows on the counter and cried. As the tears came, Sarah Goldschmidt's thoughts began to flow. A cousin who was in the *Sûreté* came to mind. She straightened up and reached for the phone directory, flipped the pages, made a note and asked the operator for the number. She could still see the recent visitor through the window as he walked towards the *Seine*. The receipt for the treasures left still lay on the countertop. His address which he had penned in neat script, was all she needed to tell her cousin. Sarah clenched her fist open and shut, open and shut, open and shut, as she waited for the line to respond.

*   *   *

Tonight she would take a different route, one hardly if at all, familiar to her and after only a short distance, there he was, standing against the river's balustrade. Smiling. He gave a short bow and, unbelievably she found herself linking arms and striding along the railing of the Seine embankment, exchanging views-how strange it all seemed in her mind-and presently-it could have been a half hour or ten minutes-she could not keep track of the time, only his presence, insistently pulling her along, yet she went willingly, wondering why this was so, she urgently felt that she must resist but her will was weak and she did not. Then, there it was. To their left, across the river Seine, above the Sacre Couer the moon, full and round and yellow, so yellow she was reminded of the custard pies her mother made all those years ago.

"We should sit here and watch," he offered.

"Here, let me lift you up."

"No, you go first, then I'll follow," she replied.

He did this and sat facing her, then in quick succession, too quick for her to comprehend, he lifted his legs up and swung on his buttocks to face the river, dropping his legs over the balustrade. She felt no feeling in her hands as she shoved all her weight against his shoulders and pushed him.

He turned his head, his open mouth revealing teeth grimacing terror and emitting a scream that was soundless, his arms flailing as he plunged into the dark swirl of the Seine. She leaned over the balustrade and watched his panic-waving arms sink out of sight.

The honking of a Taxi two floors below awoke Sarah from the nightmare. She stared momentarily at the ceiling and leaned over to the night table and reached for a cigarette.

*   *   *

Chapter 15

Perrigort travels to Rennes, a fall day in nineteen-sixty-four

Perrigort settled into his seat. The bus's heat fans quickly drowsed him. He wrestled his way out of his raincoat and pressed his face against the window. He stared blankly at the drenched, mossy velour of the artichoke fields rolling by until, quite gradually, the face of the women descending from the bus imposed on his mind. Staring, unseeing at the seatback in front of him he wondered: why would she, of all people, reappear in his life, now, on this particular day? His mind agitated fragments from their mutual lives: the squinty eyes, sunken within rings of mascara; the mouth: cupid-bowed, lip-rouged in mauve; over-rouged cheeks covering a roadmap of a life filled with wrong turns. But beneath, an unmistakable presence. It had been years, more than twenty, but yet his mind, as if recalling a long-unused phone number, had retrieved her identity; human fractions from the past — his and hers. Then she had been younger, perhaps ten years, but today, a haggard old face had replaced the erotic youthfulness of decades past. Outside, a storm enclosed the undulating fields of artichokes and the bus sluced through the drenching rain. Perrigort dozed off.

Shuffling foot steps and coats brushing against the back of his seat awakened him as the passengers clustered in the aisle. The bus had arrived at the *Rennes* rail station. He took his brief case in hand and got off and went to choose a small refractory table where he sat and placed his brief case at his feet. He ordered a cognac. Again, the day's earlier encounter invaded. Momentary re-enactments of their first entrancement flashed: the fevered sexual intensity, nights in the small railroad hotel, her bewildered, betrayed expression at her trial; all darted about in his mind as he sat.

She walked toward him, down a narrow pathway that led from the field hospital and close past the station's outdoor refectory. A leather purse with long straps swung from her shoulder. Instantly transfixed, he watched from his refectory chair. A licentious perfume wafted from her chiffon sleeves. He started to get up to follow, but at that instant a German officer appeared from around the corner. The German's youthfulness was set off by his customary polished boots and the black collar of his gray tunic. She threw her arms about his neck and rested her chin on his shoulder. As they embraced, they turned in a way that left her facing Perrigort. In fact, he realized she was staring directly at him, unsmiling, but provocative. The couple sat down at a nearby table. They each leaned forward, their heads nearly touching. She kept her hands on the tabletop while he toyed with the Iron Cross pinned to his tunic. They spoke in whispers and suddenly pulled back, bursting with laughter.

A waitress appeared, and the pair ordered. Soon, a carafe was brought, and they sipped without looking away from each other's eyes — that is, when she was not stealing glances over the officer's shoulder. At first, Perrigort believed her roaming glances to be accidental. But, as the first half hour passed into a full hour and that hour into the beginning of another, he realized the stolen looks that now lingered were intentional. He grew convinced of her interest when, fussing with her companion's epaulet, she winked over his shoulder at Perrigort.

Presently, he was seated closer the two. A train had arrived, and a large party had disembarked and demanded table service. After some discussion, the restaurateur, to make room, had approached Perrigort and offered to move his table closer to the one with the officer and the lady. Two more tables were brought out and set with tableware. Now, just centimeters from the couple, Perrigort found himself tantalized by her perfume, mesmerized by her words. He was embarrassed, like an intruder forced to listen to an intimate family conversation. He buried his eyes in office papers, but periodic squeals of laughter contravened, and he found himself compelled to listen.

"I've got to go to one of our units tomorrow. It will take most of the day."

"Where?"

"Roscoff. Where we met."

"When will you return?"

"Two days. In the evening."

"So, I have to be lonely?"

"You won't be lonely. There are all those soldiers in the hospital tents."

"What am I supposed to do with them, read them fucking Thomas Mann? Why can't you send someone else to do whatever it is?"

"General Kleist wants me to design some new field positions near Landernau. It's my duty. And he's my superior."

"That's a bad road, the one between Morlaix and the south. Tell your driver to be careful. It could be dangerous, especially in the dark."

"Silly miächen. We Germans don't believe in danger. For us, it doesn't exist."

After he paid the bill, they stood and clung together in a lingering kiss. They parted, still holding each other's hands and he slowly turned and strode toward the parking area. Her hand arced in a discrete wave as his staff car drove away.

Perrigort made note of the conversation and the license number of the car: OKW 742. He would pass the information to his cousin Tavernier, who farmed artichokes near Roscoff and always seemed to be interested in the activities of the German oc-

cupiers. As Perrigort looked up from his note taking, he met her direct, intent stare. She smiled and shrugged as if to send her perfume — Gerlain's "My Sin" — in his direction. He knew he couldn't stop himself. He moved to her table, tipped his hat and bowed and sat. They ordered a carafe. An hour later, he nervously trailed her into the small hotel across from the station.

A Paris train slowed to a stop and returned Perrigort to reality. As he reached for his briefcase, her name still eluded recall.

*   *   *

Claude Tavernier's farm, near Roscoff, October six, nineteen-forty-two

"Claude, Claude!" she shouted down the short stairway to the root cellar. "It's that fellow, again. On the phone. The one who never leaves his name? He said it's important."

A man's voice emanated from the earth-covered mound.

"Qu'est qu'il a parle?"

"He hardly spoke. He never does. He was calling from a bistro. I could hear music and people clinking glasses in the background. All he would say was that he wants to borrow your tools."

Her husband's hands appeared from under the short doorframe. He was wiping them with a cloth. He continued to wipe them as he ducked through the opening, mounted the steps, and made his way to the house.

"Make me a *baguette*," he called over his shoulder.

"Supper is almost ready."

"I haven't time for supper. Just a baguette; ham with mustard."

She cursed as she followed him into the small stone house with the carved doorframe that spelled, in timeworn lettering, "Tavernier."

She kicked off her wooden sabots before stepping down onto the tile floor. He already stood at the black phone on the wall, ringing a number.

"Shrike?" he shouted into the phone.

She could hear the scratchy responses broadcast from the earpiece.

"Le méchanicien?"

"Yes."

"I've been having trouble with my car. It keeps acting up."

"Can you bring it in?"

"That is difficult. I'm on the road a lot. Can you possibly come over?"

"Of course. Tonight?"

"No. Not tonight. I have to use it and trust to luck; but tomorrow, around dark"

"Where should I go?"

"The road from *Landernau to Morlaix*."

"There are two roads. Which one?"

"The paved one. It's the field with the goat shed, just past the stone bridge. Be careful. The new tourists have planted strange stuff around."

"Is it a Peugeot?"

"Certainly not. I wish it were. It's one we didn't used to see too much. An Adler."

"I understand. License number?"

"OKW 742."

Tavernier made note that license designated a German Staff car, *Oberkomando Wehrmacht*. "I may need parts. What's it doing?"

"It seems to run well. But then, at high speed, it cuts out for no reason at all. I would like to slow it down, if you understand what I mean. You should be in the field above the embankment, probably just after sundown."

Tavernier was about to acknowledge the assigned spot, but, before he could speak, the line went dead. He was used to that with calls from the Shrike.

"I will have supper. I have to do something first, though."

He slipped on his sabots and disappeared out the doorway.

Back in the root cellar, he lit a candle. In its flickering glow, he hefted two one-hundred-kilo sacks from the potato pile. Next, he dislodged three stones from the exposed wall. From the cavity beyond, he pulled out an oblong wooden box. The lid of the box pivoted on its hinges; inside, the dusty barrel of a machine gun glistened dully. He lifted the stock, inspected the mechanism, and then pulled the loading breach. Once released, it snapped back into place. All was well. He replaced the gun in the box, the box in the wall, and the stones and potato sacks to their usual places. When he had finished, he blew out the candle and returned to the house.

He found her huddled at the table, her shawl wrapped around her shoulders. She had been crying, he knew.

"I have a call to make tomorrow night. So don't wait up. If I'm not home by early morning, go to your cousin's. Go across the fields, not on the road. Now, don't worry. We'll get the better of the Boche."

After he had retired and she had finished the evening's washing up, she sat at the table, opening and closing her fist as the candle, low on wick, burned itself out. Outside, an owl's insistent hoots echoed through the wood and she leaned against her arms and muffled her sobs.

*   *   *

A road near Roscoff, Brittany, October seven, nineteen-forty-two

Renauld Penze peddled his bicycle over deep ruts that late-September rains and horse-drawn wagons had etched into the dirt of the back road. The pack on his back dug into his ribs at every jolt. A kilometer remained for him to traverse. He was concerned that he would not have enough daylight to finish his work. The fingers of gold sky on the horizon had begun withdrawing and the autumn darkness would descend.

He had hardly shifted his gaze from the golden streak than the wheel hit upon a sharp stone bottomed in a pothole. The front tire popped and exhaled. He cursed. There wasn't time to stop, and, he kept on because he had no patches or pump and knew – everyone knew – that the victory ahead would be worth it. He was convinced that he would soon be back in his machine shop, tinkering and fixing like he did before the Germans interrupted his usual life.

At the dirt path's intersection with a paved roadway, he got off the crippled bike and wheeled it access a ditch and into the shadows formed by low stone hedge wall. From there he strained to see if others were on the road or at the nearby bridge. He breathed a sigh of relief upon seeing no one in the falling darkness. He abandoned the bike and set about his task.

His instructions were await a low-flying plane and, at a precise moment, light a series of flares to signal a drop-zone for medical supplies and signal equipment. he set about the task as the diminishing light signaled difficulties, one traveling down the road, fifteen minutes away. He laid down a large metric area of signal wire and planted the flares at intervals of fifteen paces, counted off as he slogged through the damp soil. Almost entirely by feel, he attached wires in a series and then lead the detonation cable back to the wall and connected the lead to the hand-cranked generator. By the time he finished, a mere sliver of a crescent moon pierced the gloom. He leaned against the wall and lit a *Galois* and drew it in and exhaled, to wait. He would be glad when it was all over.

From the glen at the far end of the field came the pungent scent of wet sycamore, gingko and elm leaves. The ground creatures signaled their evening accords and a distant cowbell rang eerily. Penze listened for the sound of the plane's engine. An hour - seeming two - passed.

Then the ground creatures soundings halted, as if on signal. Then he heard it. The plane's low buzzing. With alarm, he tensed. It wasn't a plane, but a motor car approaching at high speed. He reasoned it to be German since the French weren't allowed petrol or permission to drive at night. He stood and then stepped over the wall and into the road to catch a beam of the headlamps and judge the car's distance up the road.

He thought of how he might have wired a roadside explosive and then detonated it just as the hated *Boche* came by. But there was not time for that now. Then, to his alarm, he heard the distant drone of the plane. There was no time to light the flares. He froze between his duty and his curiosity. And, then, the German staff car was suddenly upon him. He flung himself down in the ditch. In the darkness, in his haste, in his concentration to finish his assignment, he had missed the ACHTUNG MINEN sign hanging from the fencing, warning against the minefield. The explosion detonated as the staff car passed by. Stray pieces of the late Maquis section chief Renaud Penze sailed toward the car and clotted against the windscreen.

Inside the car, Kapitan Klaus Berwald, en route to Landernau, gripped the crucifix Louise had given him.

"Christ, what was that?"

"Shall I stop, Kapitan?"

"No. Drive on. The bridge approach is mined. It was probably an animal. Just get out of here. You can wash it off in the morning. A rabbit, I suspect. Tomorrow —." The trigger finger of potato-farmer cum Maquis-saboteur, Claude Tavernier, completed Berwald's sentence for him. A burst of machine gun bullets smashed through the side door, the neck of the driver and Berwald's chest. The staff car caromed off an embankment and overturned, momentarily startling a Holstein cow dreaming in a neighboring field.

As though shielding itself from an obscenity, the crescent moon vanished behind a cloud. The overturned staff-car's wheels spun slowly to a stop. Maquis leader Penze's wristwatch, its face covered with blood, still clung to his severed wrist, like a faithful dog that would not leave a dying master, ticking out living minutes its owner would never pass.

Tavernier packed up his machine gun while debating whether or not to risk examining the minefield in the dark. In truth, he didn't want to know what had caused the explosion before he opened fire. The ground creatures resumed their chatter, and the Holstein went back to its dreams. Inside the car, Louise Vernet's crucifix — her initials etched on its back — slipped from Berwald's hand. In the following weeks and months, it would hold interest for *S.S.* officials and, after V.E. Day, the French Ministry of Justice.

*   *   *

Late afternoon that nineteen-sixty-four day at the Rennes rail station

Perrigort sat at a table in the outside station bistro. He pulled a notebook out of a briefcase that rested on the floor by his feet. The case had belonged to his late father and was part of ineradicable memories of the man. Perrigort remembered the case standing at attention on the sidewalk outside his primary school as his father, a government inspector, waited at the curbside. He remembered the case at his father's side at the cold soccer field as he and his classmates exchanged adrenalin-laced taunts ("Your mother fucks turtles."); as they jockeyed for advantage ("You kicked me, I'll have your balls!"); as they found success ("Your old man lost his in the war!"); and as they celebrated their exultant triumph ("You piss-sacks shouldn't have left your tricycles at home!"); so many breathless soaring triumphs! He remembered another time: his father on a rail platform in an autumn mist, hugging the broken-handled briefcase to his chest as he waited for his son's return from a school day-trip. And, then, as his thoughts took him back, there was the day the briefcase sat alone by the front door, like a faithful spaniel, or an icon of death, as the family filed by on their way home from the hospital and his father's last illness.

Now, towards the end of his day-long return from Roscoff, he reflected on the briefcase, this symbol of adulthood and patriarchal authority and, even, of his own role in French society: a compartment for a working file, a compartment for blank paper, a compartment for personal and family matters — everything in its place. Somehow, the briefcase subtended their small, *cul-de-sac-bound,* one-and-one-half story, granite block house with its con-forming black shutters. Indeed, this briefcase evoked the transportable, frag-mentary nature of his official life, transient and transitory, with memorized segments of humanity materializing, fleetingly, then appearing briefly and then vanishing in milliseconds like birds blown about in a summer storm. He won-dered how his little grandson must see him and the family briefcase. Did the boy have thoughts similar to his own boyhood memories of the family patri-arch and the ever-present, bureaucratic, class-bound briefcase?

He sipped the cognac. The station waiter, a smudged white apron telling of an already long day approached with a menu and signaled a choice. But Perrigort wasn't hungry. He waved the man off. The retreat of the waiter somehow set off another memory, of the old woman descending from the bus at the Roscoff cemetery. All the encounters in the harbor town had randomly woven in and out of his consciousness during his trip home — the puzzled countenance of Madame Gaspard, the hotelkeeper's wife that morning: the graves of the men he was seeking — Castaignet and the strange game with the bank accounts in *Rennes.* How could it possibly be, as the bank manager had confided, that the accounts had remained inactive ever since a substantial sum was withdrawn some years before? He would have to talk to Monsieur Gaspard to see what it was all about.

Then, suddenly, like catching sight of an unexpected bolt of lightning during a summer walk in the forest, her name, from all those years before: Louise. Louise Vernet. The old woman getting off the bus in Roscoff *was* Louise. But how could she look so old? There was very little age difference be-tween them when they first met? Why had she-the girl and her German friend-hidden for decades in his memory with no recall until now?

*   *   *

Chapter 16

She looked up from the reception desk to see a man and a woman in front of the hotel emptying an oversize sedan. He was short and paunchy and dressed in a turquoise shirt covered with orange palm fronds. On the back of his tropical shirt, two monkeys held a banner flocked with silver dust; the banner spelled out "PARADISE ISLAND." It bespoke "dedicated tourist." His wife's blouse matched his. She tucked it in while shifting her weight from one hip to the other, somehow unable to decide how to help her husband. A crack of thunder drew Catherine Gaspard's attention away from her paper work and out of doors.

He pulled a suitcase from the boot and put it on the walk and turned to retrieve another as two small girls in dirndls sprang out, one a mere tot and the other aged four or five. As they skipped about, he unloaded two more suitcases and two small dog carriers from which unseen terriers emitted high-pitched yelps. He made one final dive into the car and pulled out a folded playpen.

It was the playpen that convinced Catherine that these foreign beings were the Americans she was expecting; Europeans got along without such things, she reasoned. In fact, she wondered why the family had bothered to leave home at all since they seemed to have brought all their belongings with them.

She was about to offer to help them when she happened to see Jules approaching stolidly from the direction of the city center with a sheaf of leaflets clasped to his chest. The papers flopped about as he trudged along, perilously near to cascading to the ground. Catherine hurried to the lobby door and gathered the leaflets from him. She nodded to the arriving guests, indicating that she would help if her hands were not suddenly full.

"Come inside before it rains," she called out. She fussed with her son's hair, brushing the unruly pile to one side, but the wind immediately redistributed it. He winced while staring vacantly at the Americans.

"Now, where did you go with these, *mon cher?*"

"At the crossroads leading to *Morlaix* and *Leshaven.*"

"You were gone a long time."

"Then I went to *Morlaix.*"

"To *Morlaix?*" She voiced a sudden incredulity. *"Mon cher,* how?"

"The man who drives the wine truck from there was going back for another load. I had time in *Morlaix* to put some signs up by the river walk. I put up some along the riverbank and some more by the rail station."

"Que merveilleux! Now, attend to the cat box and then wash for dinner. Your father will be home in an hour. Perhaps he has some news."

She nudged Jules toward their private quarters then helped the American guests bring their bags and children through to the foyer.

"Bienvenu, Madame. Bienvenu, Monsieur. Vous-étes les Américains, non?" She quickly had their reservation in hand. Once registered, they followed her to the stairs. She carried two bags herself. The kennels would have to be left in the garden. Outside, a sharp *Breton* gust carried one of the posters of Jean-Baptiste through the air and pasted it against a windowpane of the lobby. The leaflet clung tenaciously to the glass. Jean-Baptiste's image peered warily into the reception room.

Catherine descended the stairway to the reception desk and finished the Americans' registration form. A bolt of lightning drew her attention as it flashed across the harbor. She barely caught its afterglow in the window—as well as Jean-Baptiste's haunted face peering through the glass. Startled, she hastened to the window.

"Jean-Baptiste! Jean-Baptiste!"

It was a momentary fiction. A cruel gust plucked Jean-Baptiste's face from the pane and wafted it upward and out beyond the harbor wall. She turned back to the counter where, her head on her arm and sobbed.

*   *   *

Fall, nineteen-eighty, a bus en-route to Morlaix from Roscoff

The bus had crawled through gently rolling artichoke-cloaked fields for a seemingly endless time. A coastal fog rolled in from the sea darkening the interior, turning the windows into mirrors. Its headlights sliced into the fog-shrouded coastal road, like a weevil tunneling through bales of cotton.

At *Morlaix,* another hour's wait for the local train that would carry her and the baby to *Rennes.* There she would make another change for her journey to Paris' *Montparnasse* station. The train arrived a half-hour late; she labored the baby and her suitcase up three iron steps and found a vacant, slatted wooden bench, opposite an unkempt bearded old man, slumped deep in slumber. She settled in for the two hour journey. The baby fretted and let out a cry of hunger. She bared her breast which he took eagerly and, once satiated, fell immediately to sleep. The journey seemed much longer than two hours. Gently she put the baby down beside her on a cushion brought for the trip. The train jolted to a start and slowly got up to speed, forty-five kilometers per hour. Needing toileting, she went down the aisle of soundly sleeping passengers in search of the toilet. She found it at the end of the car, but it had a sign on the door that it was out of order. The second-class car immediately behind was locked; third-class passengers were not allowed in the sacrosanct second-class. Desperate, she knelt down on the shifting metal plates between the cars and quickly lowered her underclothes. She took care of her needs and got up, adjusted her clothing and returned to where the baby lay asleep. At one in the morning the train crept into *Rennes*. She carried the baby in one arm and her valise with the other and made her way down the carriage steps to a bench and sat, to wait for the train that would complete her trip to Paris. The engine shrilled noisily and spun its wheels as it plunged into the dark. She clutched the baby under her coat and dozed off. A time later she was awakened from her half-sleep by the shrill whistle of the locomotive, its massive, spoked wheels halted opposite her. She strode quickly to a third-class coach immediately behind the steam-panting locomotive. As she swung her case onto the car's platform the engine belched off a humid cloud of cindered-steam as the engineer, leaning out of the engine window towards the rear of the train, pulled the whistle cord for two short blasts, warning of emanate departure. She grabbed the angled railing and pulled herself up the three iron steps into the carriage. Finding a vacant slatted seat, she settled herself and the baby for the five hour journey.

She sat, leaning her head against the cold glass of the window. Unable to sleep, she stared through her reflection to the darkened fields, punctuated from time-to-time by a highway crossing light, at other times when the train crept into a village station, lit by a solitary extended lamp projecting from the wall, showing the rectangular station name, its paint faded from years of neglect. At some places a solitary trainman stood, holding a lamp level with his head, signaling only what trainmen would know. Sometimes the train would stop and a solitary trio of passengers would step from the darkness pantomiming a stage mystery and board, clutching suitcases-usually two in hand and a third secured precariously under an arm. The trainman would then hold a large circular sign at the end of a pole, the sign being green when held aloft telling the engineer he was free to steam forward onto its journey.

The baby fretted and fell asleep. The journey seemed longer than the five hours, but as kind fortune would have it, the train arrived on time. As it slowed to *Montparnasse's* glass covered platforms, relieved that the ride was over, she freshened her make-up, exhilarated that in moments she would be rejoining her lover Antoine. She hastened along the platform to a large hanging clock and stood, suitcase at her feet, looking expectantly about, hoping to gain a glimpse of him. Standing for several minutes and weary from holding the baby, she picked up the suitcase and went into the vast terminal and found a seat. The concourse, teaming with travelers pushing, anxiously scanning train departure signs, fetching breakfast baguettes from kiosks; a *mélange* of fervor she had never experienced in her small town. The immediacy of being rejoined with her lover, rushed exhilaration within her and she flushed with expectation, her feet dancing in place, shifting, heel, toe right, heel left, toe right, heel left.

She had chosen a seat affording views of several directions, the food service area, three arched doors fronting the main street, and of the concourse, itself to her front. Fifteen minutes went by. Still she waited, dancing, turning her head, watching for his swaggering gate, yearning, every moment, her head brimming with an interior ballet of eroticism and, intermittently, the realization that *Roscoff* was to be a life time behind and that she was at a new beginning.

Another quarter of an hour passed, merging to a half, to an hour; then two. Her gaze shifted to the ceiling as she recalled images from the beginning of the romance, a magic day on the beach at *Roscoff:*

I didn't know if you would come.
Actually, I thought-afraid-it might be the other way around.
I've been here a half hour.
A half hour?
Yes. I-I thought of coming earlier, myself but,
He lay facing her on his side, propped up on one elbow.
I didn't know if you had even noticed me, before.
Of course I noticed you. On the soccer field. You were standing in front of me slurping down all that water—like a stallion.
Was that the time, the first time and not at the glass shop?
No. It was at the soccer field.
He reached out and brushed back her hair, wet from the swim in the shallows of the harbor.
Your eyes are very blue, not just ordinary blue but very blue.
Both my parents have blue eyes; my three brothers, also. It's not supposed to be. The bathing suit; its turquoise. I'll bet it it's not from here.
No, of course not. It's from Paris. I ordered it from a catalogue.
I like what it doesn't show.
He put his hand on her shoulder and smiled, revealing his perfectly matched teeth. She wanted to melt. Something gave way within her.
Are you in school?
Yes. My last year at gymnasium. I haven't seen you there.
No and you won't. I dropped out. I have a good job with Monsieur LeBlanc.
The plumber?
Yes. School is for idiots who can't do anything with their hands.
His index finger traced around her neck and moved slowly down to the top of her breast as he spoke,
I like to do things ...with...my hands.
His finger slipped gently under the strap.

He leaned forward and put his lips at the top of her breast and kissed, then drew back. The incoming tide sloshed at their feet.

Her eyes glowed and she whispered,

You can do ... more, if you want.

Again the tide brushed conspiratorially at their naked limbs and washed the calves of their legs.

He reached over her head, his arm covering her mouth as he reached for his watch. Startled he pulled away from her and sprang up.

It's almost noon; I told Monsieur LeBlanc I'd pick up a load of piping from the station in Morlaix at two. I've got to scram.

Jumping up, he pulled on his trousers over his wet suit and in a hoarse whisper said, "I'll be back."

He sprang away as she looked after his retreating figure, her heart being borne away by his every stride. Irene started to call after him, but her throat choked up and no words came out. She pressed her hand against her breast where he had touched.

*   *   ·   *

She followed the aged woman up the wooden steps, circling a caged elevator that no longer worked. At the landing between the first and the second floors she paused, breathing heavily and asked,

"When you said the rent was 'reasonable', Madame, how much, is 'reasonable'?" Demurring a direct answer, the old woman replied "the location is very convenient; *rue Lepic* has everything, like a village unto itself ! Just wait until you see it, Mademoiselle, what was your name again, dear? I get forgetful; I'm seventy-two."

"Irene. Irene Gaspard" she answered as she turned the landing-the third in a climb that would convey her to her new home, under the watchful eyes of the Saints residing in spirit form in the imposing edifice of *Sacre Cover,* gazing benignly over the entire of Paris. She still broiled with anger, despair and confusion leading to the reality of her betrayal and abandonment. Steeling herself, she would not cry. Not at the present; perhaps later but not now. It might confuse the old lady leading her up, her rubber-toed cane thumping against each step. It would look bad and besides it might interfere with her bargaining for the apartment she had seen advertised, hand written and papered on a post near *Montparnase.* Now, the climb progressively wearied. Her mind drifted as they took a moment to rest, the old woman chattering on. It was the last milestone in a seemingly endless journey from Roscoff.

"Gaspard? I knew a Gaspard once. Some time ago. A young man. He only stayed a month and got behind in the rent. The flicks came looking for him a week after he vanished. Strange."

Roscoff; still the images: the stealth of stepping from her parent's hotel into an evening fog rolling in from the harbor; the Belle-époque lighthouse beam following her figure, the horn mournfully sounding farewell. And the endless waiting for Antoine at Montparnase and trudging up the steepness of rue Lepic from Métro

Blanche and the red blades of the Moulin Rouge waving her into her new Parisian life.

At this moment, all Irene knew was that she was tired, very tired and so when the old lady unlocked the door revealing the raw beams and the steep angled roof she took a quick look about and realized it was workable, if only the price?

"He was from some place on the coast; I just can't remember...are you getting tired? We can rest. I'm sure you will like it. It's only one floor above the W. C. and I have just put in a new shower on the third floor, always with a good supply of hot water, only twenty centimes each use. It's very reliable. Now, the surprise I have been waiting to show you."

The old lady turned pridefully as she beckoned Irene, backing along the raw, planked floorboards past a pot-bellied stove towards a dormer window a few inches above head-level. A wooden ladder-backed chair stood in the space offered by the window. The old lady pointed to the chair,

"Now you just climb up there and see what a view you have, of *Le Tour!*"

Irene, tired but ever polite, dutifully climbed the chair. What she saw didn't convey immediate ecstasy. Beneath, a steep blue-gray, Mansard slate roof, clustered with pigeon droppings, splotched in *avant-garde* mode to the guttering, below. To the left of this *vue ordinaire*, a chimney spiked six clay pipes skyward, exhausting smoke into the gray Parisian skies.

To the left of the chimney, was a meter-wide gap between the roof of her soon to be new domicile, (she already had made the decision to let the space) and the nearby building of the same vintage and degree of dissolute gray. Beyond, angled acres and acres of that very same slate, sheltering the enormity of *Paris*.

Her mind traveled to kiosks and spindles of tourist-enticing post cards, adorned with seas of these same roofs. She continued to stand, her head poking out of the roof like a prairie gopher. Putting her thoughts together, a wanting for this particular piece of slate shelter, bird droppings and all, grew. It would give her and her infant son, Georges, shelter from the fall rains, the first tentative drops at that very moment commencing to fall. She was about to withdraw into the attic and step down, when she saw, between the dual architectural distress, a very distant roofline beyond which she perceived was the cause of the old lady's ecstasy: the minaret-like tip-no more than that, only the tip-of the *Tour de Eiffel*.

Her mind, mixed with want and caution and still calculating, she stepped down and flashed a hesitant half-smile and asked the price. The old woman's reached up for her glass beaded necklace. Her blue-veined hand traveled the beads as she cleared her throat and gutteraled a price. Irene, trained in street bargaining, stood mock-stunned, a look of ravaged disappointment stealing across her face. She slumped in dejection and wordlessly went toward the suitcase by the chair where the child lay sleeping. She picked up the infant and the suitcase and moved toward the door, saying,

"I'm sorry to have taken your valuable time, it is much too—" She put her hand on the door handle, before turning to finish her sentence, "much, too much, too much." The last few words, barely audible, artfully quavered from her throat.

She raised her chin from her chest where she had studiously let it fall and let out a slight whimpering, hurt spaniel sigh, whispering,

"I'm sorry, Madam; I'm just a poor country girl and the city is perhaps too expensive, no?" It's nice, *trés trés bon, trés* what I wanted but too expensive, both for the baby and myself." She raised the baby slightly toward the old lady as she continued, "I thank you for showing it, both for the baby and myself."

She pulled at the door. The old lady spoke,

"But wait! Perhaps we can have an arrangement!" she urged, lurching forward to close the door.

Irene paused and slowly turned. Later she would recall it was one of her best dramatic pieces, unequalled by Mistinguet, Bernhardt, Piaf or any of the other theatric greats.

"How much can you afford, Mademoiselle...Gaspard?

Irene remained at the door, frozen. A long minute and, again,

"Mademoiselle... Gaspard?"

Irene knew she had won, before she opened her mouth to reply.

*   *   *

Chapter 17

Rennes, the office of Tax Authority Jean Perrigort, nineteen-sixty-five

"Our examiners are saying that your income was much greater than you declared, Monsieur Gaspard. I have their figures here, against the ones you submitted. For instance, they state that the income derived from the hotel was almost six times what you declared, and from your law practice it was seven times what you stated. You can imagine that the authorities expect that you, as a lawyer, would have full possession of facts and documents to file an accurate return."

"But, Madame LaGrande did the preparation. I thought it would look better, to have another person do it. She kept all the books and was in possession of all the facts. Much of my time was spent in visiting with clients, attracting new ones, but the everyday details I left to Madame LaGrande."

"According to the figures they have, your account in the bank in *Rennes* had almost two million francs deposited in it, during the year in question."

"I don't have an account in *Rennes*. I have one in *Morlaix,* though."

"Let me show you this photo of the records. Is this your signature, Monsieur Gaspard?"

He studied the document and then looked up, astonished.

"It is close. But, I don't think it is mine."

"I don't understand, Monsieur Gaspard. It is either your signature or it is not your signature."

"It's not my signature."

"And the withdrawal signatures of 4,200,000 francs from this account, these are not yours, either? They appear to be the same."

"Perhaps Madame LaGrande can explain, only, I don't know where she is. She disappeared a few weeks ago. She left a note saying she would be gone for a week to care for a sick relative. But she hasn't returned. I don't know why."

Perrigort put the papers into a folder lying on the desk. He clasped his hands under his chin and eyed Sargan Gaspard as one would a felon.

"May I ask you, Monsieur Gaspard, do you have any other properties that you let out, regularly?"

"No, Monsieur. In fact, I don't own the hotel. I signed it over to my wife some time ago."

"Do you gamble? That is, for large sums of money?"

"No, Monsieur."

"Have you an acquaintanceship with one Alois Castaignet?"

"Not the slightest, Monsieur, though the name is familiar."

"Or one Fleur Saint-Eustace?"

"There are people with that name still in Roscoff. But, no," he responded, somewhat puzzled. "Should I know these people?"

"I would think so."

As Gaspard watched Perrigort pull more sheaves of papers from another file on the desk, he unconsciously pulled at his moustache, his growing nervousness having at last erupted to the surface, amid withering feelings of sitting between two paranoids in a darkened cinema.

"These are checks for ten-thousand francs, checks made out from your account to each of Monsieur Castaignet and Madame Saint-Eustace and endorsed to the account you say you don't have in *Rennes*. There are over fifty of these checks. A lot of money, wouldn't you agree?"

"I'm sure Madame LaGrande can explain. May I call you when she returns?"

"Of course. But, it should be soon, Monsieur Gaspard. And I wouldn't make any long-distance travel plans."

"I understand."

On his way to the railway station, Sargan repeated the sums in his head. He was genuinely at a loss. He had believed the settlement for the matter of the child, Jean-Baptiste, was generous. A cold hollow opened inside him. It remained as he boarded the train that would take him back to *Morlaix* and *Roscoff*. The chill grew as he contemplated the possibility that Joline LaGrande may not have been satisfied with fifty-thousand francs.

Back in *Roscoff*, he entered the back door of their small hotel. At their rooms, just off the lobby, he had his second surprise of the day. The door was locked, and his key didn't work. He found a note penned in his wife's hand in the jamb of the door: "Ashes to ashes and dust to dust, here is the 'forever' you promised, just." Below was inscribed a house number down the street, off the strand, a house his parents once owned. He was to move back to its cold attic. Generously, he would be allowed to use the small lavatory by the reception desk of the hotel.

He climbed the stairway and opened the door to the beam-exposed roof. A single over-stuffed chair, once colored maroon and its color faded and fabric worn, stood in the middle of the room. A narrow bed with a thin mattress was placed under the single window overlooking the harbor. He turned on the floor lamp. One of its frosted shaded bulbs came alit. The others remained dark. Slowly, he stripped to his underwear and placed his shirt and trousers on the chair relic, and lay on the bed. The springs sagged under his weight and he pulled the tattered woolen coverlet up to his neck and stared up at the rafters. A strand of moonlight lit his somber ambience. Staring into the dimness he recalled an earlier time:

Sargan Gaspard, nineteen and new to feeling the joys of life, was in the family attic with Catherine, two years younger than he and, for a few more minutes, virginal. The two had gone to the attic to hang out an American flag because the dreaded Boche had but two weeks before been routed from the pill box fortification at the harbor. Catherine's interest had commenced two years before when she and her friends at the convent school had gone to a soccer match. Sargan had stood at a water spigot piped up from the grounds, gulping down a prodigious amount of liquid as she pretended not to watch. When he had finished, he straightened up and looked at her and smiled. The other girls at the school wouldn't let it rest, and, so, Catherine, never one to wait for anything, contrived a meeting at the cinema in Morlaix. There, over a period of time, now grown vague in her mind, subsequent gropings had contrived their present tryst in the attic. He remembered hiding himself behind a family photo album and her reaching for it and finding something more interesting than the pictures.

Weeks later, after the weekly cinema, the two locked eyes in a brasserie. He pressed a gold chain into her hands.

"Forever?" he whispered.

"Forever," she replied, though he wasn't sure that she meant it, that day or any other time they met in the following years. Somehow, he felt, she was always contriving the next step.

*   *   *

Chapter 18

Roscoff, 21, rue du Quay, a morning in nineteen-seventy

The stairs were unusually steep, and the youth concentrated keenly to keep the black lacquer tray level as he climbed up. The tray held a porcelain coffee pot and a plate of napkin wrapped warm *croissants*. Bringing breakfast to his aunt was his first duty each Saturday. He didn't mind. Saturdays and Sundays were his favorite days of the week. They were the days when he was sent from home to help at his aunt's flower stall. His name was Melville Saint-Eustace, and the house, at number 21, *rue du Quay,* was home to his widowed aunt, Fleur Saint-Eustace. He had already been up for an hour, having risen from the sleeping couch in the small living room and having washed his face in the small basin in the kitchen before darting down the narrow street to the *boulangerie*. There, as always, he bought three *croissants*. His aunt's custom was to share at least one with him. Melville would take his pick, and then his aunt would choose. The third was up for grabs.

He reached the top step anxious to begin the breakfast game. As always, he began by kicking gently on the door and speaking softly.

"It's the *petit de'jeuner,* Gargoyle."

"Gargoyle" was a pet name, his aunt's contrivance. On walks through the town, she would point out gargoyles on church eaves and explain that the grotesques were little boys who had done bad things and had been cursed with transformation forever and ever, and that if he, Melville, didn't do exactly as he was told, he was in grave danger of being changed into one also. The aunt would then laugh and make a sign of the hex and tell Melville that she was exactly the one who could transform him because she was herself a witch. To prove it, she would perform some simple, mystifying magic trick. Of course, he was older now, thirteen, and he told himself that she had lost her magic powers. The fear of the hex had fallen away. The nickname remained a private joke between them. In the game, Madame Saint-Eustace was to guess what filling was in the *croissants*. If she failed to guess within three tries, Melville would have two rolls and his aunt but one. Each Saturday, his aunt would sleepily reply, "Strawberry?"

After the guessing, Melville would giggle and push open the door and go to the bedside and put the tray on the bed and then help prop pillows behind his aunt's back. He would pour her coffee into her mug, and the two would plan the day while they devoured the *croissants*.

But this morning the game played differently. He kicked at the door. His aunt did not answer. Puzzled, young Melville pushed the door aside and went to the bed.

She lay on her side, facing him, the covers pulled up to her neck.

"Ma tante, ma tante, je suis le gargoyle de la petit déjeuner."

He set a corner of the tray on the bed and placed a tentative hand on her shoulder. He quickly drew it back, realizing that Death had played his own game and that he and his aunt would never laugh over breakfast ever again. The coffee tray crashed to the floor. He ran, terrified, from the room, down the stairs and onto the street.

*   *   *

Chapter 19

Paris, Jolene LaGrande's apartment, a morning, nineteen-seventy

The copper-colored dachshund padded purposefully across the room, his thin tail wagging like a mad wand. A geranium leaf fluttering down to the carpet had excited his curiosity. He sniffed and pawed at it tentatively, then quickly lost interest. More inviting was the seat of the side chair he seemed to own. He leapt up and settled on its soft cushion and stared expectantly at his mistress.

Joline LaGrande watched with detachment. Her cigarette smoldered as she sipped at her *café latte*. She coughed, slightly at first, and then spasmodically stabbed out the *Galois* and rasped, holding her chest with one hand while applying a hanky to her mouth. The spasm stopped, and she pulled the cloth away. Blood had mixed with her phlegm, even more than she had noticed a week earlier. She must make time, she promised herself, to see her doctor.

The flap on the hallway letterbox clanked. The dog leapt to the floor and began to bark at the door. Joline forced herself from the table. She found the box filled with unwanted solicitations. She coaxed the dog, leaping at her feet, back into the apartment while she sorted the pile. On the bottom was an unexpected envelope from the friary school in *Raon L'Etape* in Alsace where she had sent Jean-Baptiste four years before. She picked up her nail file and slit the seal. The lettering, neatly formed, did not meander over the page as it had done in earlier missives. It was blocky and small. She would need her glasses.

"Dear Aunt. The food gets worse. This week I got an 'A' on my grammar and a picture of the Virgin for making my bed neat. The new boy I told you about, Georges, has been moved to the bed next to me. We now have fourteen in the room. He is good at sums. He is helping me write this. His birthday is the same week as mine. When can I come to see you? Can I bring Georges?"

She folded the letter and returned it to its envelope.

*   *   *

93

Joline LaGrande's apartment, nineteen-seventy-four

A steady draft from the kitchen's open window forced the candle's flame to lean, sending a drip down its side and onto the checkered cloth. Jean-Baptiste watched as Madame LaGrande touched the hot wax. When it had cooled on her finger, she looked across the table at the twelve-year-old. He fidgeted with his brioche then dipped it into his mug of warm milk.

"Is it time for you to be a man, Jean-Baptiste? Because, if it is time for you to be a man, even though you and I know you aren't, there are things you should know. So, I'll ask you, are you ready to be a man?"

The boy lifted the brioche and held it, dripping, over the cup. For a moment he wished he were back at the friary school in Alsace. But he looked up at her and replied, "Yes, Aunt. I am ready to be a man."

"You must remember that some things happen over which we have no control. It's God's will. Do you believe in God, Jean-Baptiste?"

"Yes, aunt."

"There has been an accident. In a car. Your mother and father are dead. They are in heaven, with the angels. It happened some time ago. I wanted to spare you, so I saved it until I thought you were a man, Jean-Baptiste."

She got up and put on her coat. She rubbed the boy's shoulder and went out. The boy stared ahead for several moments before again dipping his brioche in the milk and taking another bite. The flame of the candle flickered; more wax traveled down onto the blue checkered cloth. He reached forward and ran his finger through the warm collected tallow. The cat leaped up onto his lap and stared at him, expectantly. He stroked the cat behind its ears, looking vacantly into the room.

Outside, Joline paused outside the building's entrance and clutched her handbag tightly to her side. For a moment, she felt aimless. The impact of what she had just revealed to Jean-Baptiste absorbed her. She knew the fiction of the car accident was in some ways wrong, but the boy was happy with her and was well provided for. And she *was* the boy's mother. No one could take that away from her. *No one.* And, now, he was hers, *all* hers, with no ties to the past. And it felt good. She had won. *She had won!*

With that thought, she knew she had found her way again. She started out in a strident march as a triumphant surge of realized revenge raged through her. For once, she was in *control!*

*   *   *

Chapter 20

Paris, autumn, the nineteen-eighties

Irene Gaspard walked quickly along rue *Saint Dominique* as late twilight set-tled in. She was off to see Vernon Daumier, her lover, in *Versailles*. She was anxious to see him and just as anxious to get away from *Paris*, away from her tiny apartment in the 18th *arrondissement,* away from her job at *Gallerie LaGrande* and away from her second, part-time job — and her one-time lover — at Bernard Foucard's real estate development office. She would stop on her way, as usual, to check in on the old woman she called "Aunt" who lived across from the rail station at *Chaville*, between *Sevres* and *Versailles*. The sidewalk narrowed and Irene slowed her pace. An elderly woman was approaching, la-boring with a two-wheeled cart. To let the woman by, Irene stepped into the street but, then, as quickly, stepped back up the curb and against the nearest shop front. A moped, driven by a plastic-helmeted rider looking like a giant insect clutching a broomstick, had sliced dangerously by.

Irene caught her breath as the aged woman, her wrists, skeleton-like, wrapped in parchment skin, arthritically tapped by, muttering to herself. Irene turned away from the elderly malcontent and pressed herself against the glass. To hide her own impatience, she focused on the contents of the shop's window display — a cluster of small objects, loosely arranged on a faded green *peau de sole* covering.

She had passed by this same window every time she took the commuter train to *Versailles*. She had seen most of its baubles before — tokens of affec-tion, love and passion. A short narrow-necked *Sevres* scent bottle with pink and gold rosettes etched into white porcelain, a frosted-swan pin box — *Lalique, perhaps?* an etched crystal carafe with six matching aperitifs — awaiting new affections, new loves, new passions—often catching her eye.

But today it wasn't those that drew her interest; rather, it was a golden locket hanging by a thin gold chain from a small wooden rack. To view it better, she placed her hands against her cheeks to frame her face against the window. Filigree *fleur-de-lis* surrounded the locket: unique. Instantly, a craving livened within her. She wanted it. She *would* have it. She tried unsuccessfully to read the small price tag, upside-down, aslant. She continued to press her face to the glass as her eyes traveled the green covering, taking in the flotsam of abandoned bibelots. An oval mirror, framed in ivory, would have been held in one hand for a hundred self-inspections: *"Ah-ha!" its owner might have cooed. "A new line, cornering the eye; where did that come from? It wasn't there yesterday. Or was it? And that blemish. Can be covered up. Not now. Must hurry. Husband's waiting downstairs. Mustn't be late."* Beside it, a tortoise-shell comb-set, edged in silver and initialed; a porcelain miniature of a young girl. Where was she now? Is she still alive or did I pass by her tomb last week at *le cimetiere Montmartre?* What was her name? Monique? Or was she tending the flower stall by *d'Orsay* — old, gnarled, cheeks no longer pink?

Irene's eyes repeatedly returned to the locket, as though a force it possessed was pulling her attention with an intimate bonding power. Its shape intrigued her. Not round. Octagonal, rather. Unique. She had seen one like it somewhere. She would tell Vernon about it *and, just perhaps?* She dropped her arms and turned from the window to continue on her way to the *Métro.*

Within the shop display, the locket caught a vagrant beam from the sun, which danced against her retreating figure, portending the tragedy that it would one day bring.

✳   ✳   ✳

Chapter 21

Paris, the office of Bernard Foucard, La Defense, a morning in the nineteen-eighties

Bespoke cutting-edge art and minimalist steel-and-leather furniture evoked the higher level clientele seeking out the real estate mogul's expertise in property transactions. A less esthete passionate conversation flowed in the director's office of *Bernard Foucard et Cie,* one of France's leading real estate development firms,

"There seems to be a problem. Well, not so much a problem. More like a snag on the *avenue Salengre* project."

"A snag?"

"An impasse, perhaps?"

"An impasse? *An impasse?* Let me explain. On a hundred-million-franc project, funded in half by myself, personally, there can be no *fucking impasse.* I was under the impression that everything was firm, set in stone, final, and everything was all arranged."

"That, Monsieur Foucard, was the impression that we conveyed to the landholder of the vacant property next door in order to get title. It was, say, possibly a little deceptive, but, you will recall, we did get the adjacent property."

"So, we successfully deceived not only the dolt that we got the minor property from, but we became so entranced with our own flicking story that we deceived *ourselves! Merde!*"

"I think we can work out the problem. Under the circumstances, I thought I should advise you right away."

"What is the specific problem?"

"Two old ladies in two apartments. Unfortunately, one is the Comtesse Blanche Everon du Plais. *Monsieur le Directeur,* she is the widow of Field Marshal Philippe Renault, the hero of Verdun and a power behind the Ministry of Defense. He departed this world in 1939. As his widow, she is entitled to lifetime tenure in one of the flats of the building."

"Can't she be bought?"

"Well, 'A,' she likes the building. And, 'B,' she is conservator of a small bird sanctuary on the property."

"Can we cause the elevator to fail? Or poison the goddamn birds, or something?"

"Monsieur, the building is early eighteenth-century. There were no..."

"Yes, yes, I understand. All right, thanks."

Bernard Foucard dismissed the bringer of bad news by a slight wave of his hand and taking up a folder and spinning his chair around to face the window overlooking Paris' eastern gray expanse. His temples pulsed. Was this what he deserved? The third son a field artillery colonel, a graduate of *Saint-Cyr*, a retired major who had seen service in Algiers, a former diplomat who had turned his contacts in government into the most substantial and lucrative real estate empire in *Paris*? All to be held up in a major project by a loony widow? He pushed himself back around to his desk as his fingers drummed with Nairobian intensity, an angry tattoo on the chair arms.

*　　*　　*

Chapter 22

A hotel in the fourth arrondissement, about the same time

Antoine put a stop to the ringing of the hotel's kitchen phone.

"Service," he announced into the receiver, "of course, Madame. Right away. Decaffeinated or regular coffee?"

He hung up the receiver and grabbed a tray. He found a cup and saucer and a white porcelain pot that he filled at the small kitchen's espresso machine. He added a plate and napkin to the tray, then retrieved butter, jam and, from under a greasy towel, two tepid *croissants*. The hotel lift carried him to the third floor where he held the door for an Algerian cleaning lady. As he proceeded down the hall, he passed a room door that stood slightly ajar. He glanced behind him and rapped lightly. He waited some moments and rapped again. Cautiously, he pushed the door open, murmuring, "Service."

It would not do to have the coffee go cold, so he moved as quickly as he could, pulling the door almost closed behind him and setting down the tray on a dresser. The bath was empty. The bureau looked unused, but he tried a side drawer nonetheless. A jewel box surprised him. He popped the lid and deftly scooped up two rings, a locket and a ladies wristwatch — *Philippe Patek*. He pocketed the items and turned back to retrieve his tray. He was not prepared for the formidable, familiar figure in the doorway.

"So," the man bellowed, "you're the little snitch. I thought it might be you. Empty your pockets and put the stuff you stole back in the drawer."

"But, you're one of the cooks. Why do you care? Here, I can split it with you"

"Not a chance." The man pulled a set of handcuffs from his belt. "I'm with the police. I'm afraid both our careers here are at an end."

He pinned Antoine's hands behind his back and fastened the cuffs.

"You're a terrible cook," Antoine wagered.
"You're not much of a waiter."

*   *   *

Chapter 23

Paris, Bistro la Bretagne, some time later

Antoine kicked down the prop on his motorbike and bounded up the two front steps of *lá Bourbonaise.*

Glancing over his shoulder he noted that the tree of post cards usually set out on the sidewalk in front of the shop two doors up was nowhere to be seen. He stored the observation in his mind, noting, too, that the proprietor, a large man with a black handlebar moustache, was not sitting at his usual table.

As usual, the door scraped against the floor as he entered and then reluctantly closed, as he strode over to the bar. The proprietor had already started making his morning *café grande* as he always did when he saw the young man approaching. Antoine let the *café grande* cool — stirring it, taking a few experimental sips — while staring blankly at the Citroens sluicing along the newly rain-drenched avenue. Someday, he would own a Citroen; when he had his own company and sit at a chrome and rosewood desk in a fine office at *la Defense.*

Still sweating from the circuitous bike challenge from his narrow quarters in the twenty-third *arrondissement* public housing, itself monolithic and demeaning, he was clad in worn black corduroys. A nickel plated-what else- chain link bracelet swiveled about as he shifted on his seat, rubbing his chin, his hairline moustache in need of a trim, calling needless attention to the seahorse tattooed on his neck, wondering at what was to transpire in the meeting.

As he waited, his eyes fell upon an abandoned copy of the morning's *Le Temps* lying on the nearby barstool. He picked it up, glanced at the picture of a gory automobile accident of the previous night, and then turned to the sports pages. He clucked haughtily at the players' mistakes. He flipped more pages and read of a daring burglary in the affluent sixteenth *arrondissement*. The clock above the bar showed twenty minutes past eight.

He had been offered release from the jail weeks before and had been offered employment after a meeting in a fourth arrondissement cabaret, "The Upright" by a young business man.

He was finishing the sports section and looked up as the sleek *Citreon* slowed to a stop in the *stationnement interdit* zone. The driver-his acquaintance from a few nights before, got out and slammed the door and strode into the bistro, looked about, seeing Antoine, turned to the proprietor and ordered two coffees and approached.

"Antoine! Something to make you come alert! How are you?"

"Yes. Thank you, Monsieur Foucard, for your help. I'm going straight, now."

"Let's hope. Small-time stealing is stupid. I'll get to the point. I need your help. There will be some extra in it for you, of course. Let me explain."

The proprietor brought two coffees and left the bill.

"Merci, Monsieur," Foucard mumbled toward the proprietor's back. "Now, Antoine, the problem is that we have an elderly lady in the building that we are about to renovate. She has trouble sleeping. She's into some sort of spiritualism, and I'm really concerned about her. She has been with us as a resident for longer than Marie Antoinette. She's complained that her late husband, an old Field Marshal, is trying to communicate with her from the spirit world and that our work on the building is setting up strange vibrations and interfering with her parlays with the dead man. Don't ask me to explain the reasoning. I've tried other measures and they haven't worked".

Antoine stirred his coffee and looked questioningly. "What can I do, Monsieur Foucard?"

"You can call me 'Bernard', first of all. Since I want this to be in strict confidence, I want things on an informal basis. Now, since your work at the hotel, have you found anything?"

"No, Mon... Bernard."

"Have you ever done any construction? You can see we have some work going on here."

"Yes, I was a plumber's helper, awhile back"

A uniformed policeman suddenly loomed over their table. His approach had been so quiet that the two were equally startled at his interruption. He saluted and asked,

"Which one of you gentlemen owns the grey *Peugeot* parked outside with the lights on?"

"I do, thank you, officer. I shall turn off the lights."

"The vehicle is parked, you may have noticed, in an illegal zone."

Bernard stood and reached into his jacket pocket for a leather case. He removed a business card and handed it to the officer. The policeman glanced at the card.

"Monsieur, I must ask you to remove the car. I shall avoid a citation at this time."

"Thank you, officer. I'm lunching with the commissioner of police next week, and I shall tell him of your alertness and courtesy. Many thanks. I shall be but one more moment, thanks."

The officer nodded and turned away. Bernard sat down and resumed his instructions,

"Antoine, this is all you have to do. Tomorrow talk to the foreman on the job across the street. He'll take you on without questions. Then, once or twice a week, remain after work. Make your way to the attic above the apartment on the fifth floor, the one with the curtains. You can go up the back stairs and pull down the ladder to the attic. You'll find an instrument, a viola. It doesn't matter if you have never played one before, Antoine."

"I took lessons once. I had some trouble at school, so I quit."

"Excellent. What you do is stroke the strings softly with the bow, as tunelessly as you can. Tap your foot on the floor every now and then. Do this for about half an hour. Then leave. Make sure no one sees you go up or come down.

"It shouldn't be a problem because there are only two old ladies living in the building and one needs a chair to move about. It will give untold comfort to the Field Marshal's widow to think her husband is communicating with her. I must go. Here's a card with my private number. Perhaps an aperitif, next week? Perhaps at my apartment, if you'd like? I have some rather nice antiques I could show you?"

"That would be great, Mon... Bernard, I will let you know if I have any problems. Thanks for the opportunity. And thanks for getting me bailed out. Next week at your place would be great."

The two left the café together. Outside, Bernard slid into his *Peugeot* and revved the motor. Before he left, he rolled down the window and held out an object wrapped in black cloth.

"Here, take this. You may need it."

The *Peugeot* sped into the traffic as Antoine looked after it. Someday, he vowed, he would drive a car like that.

Antoine unfolded the cloth-wrapped bundle just handed to him. He glanced up, hoping no one had been watching him, then anxiously rewrapped the .38 Lugar and tucked the bundle under his arm as he edged toward his motor bike.

*   *   *

Chapter 24

One week later, the Bistro la Bretagne

Antoine opened the bistro door and stepped down to the crosswalk and waited for the light to change. In moments, it did and he walked briskly to the other side of the street and up to a large extension bucket. A moped squealed to a stop behind him, and two of his coworkers with black, shiny helmets closing around their heads, dismounted. They propped their vehicle against a nearby cyclone fence and came toward him.

"*Jour*, Antoine." Extended hands were shaken.

"*Jour*, Michel. *Jour*, Vincent," he replied.

"What's doing?"

"Nothing big. Grocery shopped and wrote a letter home. It's been more than ten years, but I keep in touch with my mom. She's split from my father. And you?" "We heard about a guy who is starting up a new company and wants a construction foreman."

"Are you going to try for it?"

"It's in *Lille* and I'm not prepared to move. Besides, if the company doesn't make it; who wants to be stranded in *Lille*?"

Later, during their lunch break, he ordered an extra *baguette* for his late-night snack because it was another night when he would wait for the cover of darkness and then let himself into the enclosure surrounding the ancient dwelling and ascend the stairs to the attic.

*   *   *

His fingers were again drumming when the phone rang. He glanced at his secretary beyond the glass wall of his office. Her nod indicated that the call had passed her initial screening.

"Oh, *bonjour*, Antoine. Have you found a way to solve the problem?"

His drumming fingers stalled in midair; then gripped his fountain pen.

"I agree. She is of advanced age, Antoine. And with not long to live. But each day, each hour, she's costing me too much. Simply waiting for her to die is like waiting for a *glacier* to melt. We know it will happen in time, but how much time? It's too bad that she is a Field Marshal's widow, or we could have done something legally. This is costing me a pretty *sou*. I won't tell you how much each day, but the amount that I would be willing to pay just to have the old bitch out of there would make a difference in your life. I'm not suggesting anything more than prudence. Are you a prudent man, Antoine?" He lowered his voice, and his next words were measured, menacing. "What I mean is, wouldn't fifty-thousand francs improve your lifestyle, perhaps allowing you to return to *Roscoff*?"

He listened, stabbing his pen on a notepad and scribbling.

"Oh, I had quite forgotten. *Roscoff* would be inappropriate. For many reasons. But, I have explored other options. The building is expensive to insure, so we don't want to go that way, even though fires are convenient. There's the one old lady we can boot out at anytime, leaving the old lady as the main problem. The only one. The only one separating you from fifty-thousand francs, the only one, Antoine. Think about that. *Fifty thousand francs. Au revoir, Antoine.*"

He set the phone in its cradle and examined the violent doodle he had absently drawn.

In the outer office, Irene Gaspard reached for her purse and her little black book. She did not often listen to her employer's phone calls, but she sometimes wrote down in her secret black diary what she did hear. She thought it might all be useful one day, the notes in the little black book.

What she had just heard piqued her curiosity more than most calls. She had overheard Antoine's name being used. A scheme came to mind in which Antoine might be made to regret his betrayal in the garden house behind her parent's hotel so many years before — two years before her little brother, Jean-Baptiste, had so mysteriously disappeared. She thought about what she had gone through in those dreary, mordant years between. All those years. *Years* of not enough food, the cold water attic in the 18th, the *Métro* rides crowded with Algerians on the long trip to the public health clinics, always with her son, Georges, sick with this, sick with that, `till at last she could afford his boarding school in Alsace where the nuns say he wants to become a priest. *Years* of shopping for castoff clothing until she met Bernard at the little brasserie in the 18th and what began as a two-hour affair in a third-floor walk-up hotel instead lasted all night and became an extended relationship and a part-time job that had, in the end, proved very good for her. For now, five years later, she could afford a cozy apartment off *rue de Passy* in the Sixteenth, a car, and tuition for her son, though she still had to be careful. Very careful, indeed, as she was still walking close to the edge. She smiled to herself. She knew there was at least one other who was walking close to the edge, and that was Antoine. Waiting for a shove.

Her scheme grew over the course of the day. By the time she turned off her computer and said *bon noir* to Bernard, she knew she would, of course, tell her "auntie" all about Antoine and caution her to be careful. In fact, on her way to the Metro, she even had a fleeting memory of having only recently seen someone much like Antoine at the *brasserie* on the avenue *Salengre*. What, she wondered, why was he there, young but not working?

* * *

Paris, the Brasserie La Defense, two weeks later

Bernard flipped the gold cigarette lighter between his finger and thumb, tapping it on the table at each revolution. He gazed at Antoine's hands, not his face. His speech was low, measured, and determined.

"Antoine, there was an unfortunate incident at a certain building that is of particular interest to me. A fire. It was unfortunate because there wasn't more of it, along with some foresight. Were you aware, Antoine, that half of the local fire company for the *arrondissement* was in the *brasserie* precisely across the flicking avenue from where your accidental fire occurred? It was a bachelor's party for one of the fire brigade. They even had the fire truck parked outside, decked out in cute little garlands. The only thing they didn't have was your name painted on the side — 'Guest of the Evening.' They had the fire out, in *milliseconds*. The smoke damage was minor, but, if someone had had some presence of mind, it could have conveniently — and, I might add, profitably — suffocated any of the occupants of the building. Fortunately for one of the old ladies, bless her soul, the smoke never reached her. The other was away from the building visiting her niece for the night. Her apartment sustained only smoke damage. The insurance company says that the old gal had upgraded her coverage to full replacement cost, whatever it may be. Since she has many heirloom antiques from the seventeenth century — and not, I might add, from the 1930s, as you had thought — the result, my dear genius, is that the old darling came out ahead, and we did not. In fact, we are behind because her insurance company is now suing our insurance company for costly upgrades to the building, upgrades that we have been bribing right and left not to be done. One of the improvements the insurance company wants is an elevator for the old girls. We have sixty days to start construction, unless, well, unless something else happens.

"Now, Antoine, since fires do not seem to be your métier, I have another suggestion."

106

Bernard handed his henchman a paper on which was typed an advertisement: *A nurse companion is desired for alert, bright, elderly lady of means in a fashionable live-in apartment. Vic. Versailles. Must be able to lift wheelchair. Box 6835.*

*   *   *

Chapter 25

Paris-Chaville, an apartment on avenue Salengre, nineteen-eighty

Vivian de La Roche, for many years assuming the persona of the late Countess Blanche Everon du Plais, gingerly swept her broom along the edge of the balcony, wanting to get the work done before the noonday sun grew too harsh for her tender old eyes. She brushed against a geranium as she swept. The gnarled plant dropped a leaf; she stabbed at it with her broom. The plant was one of three pillars she put out each spring and she preserved each autumn by shaking the earth off the roots and hanging to dry in her storage area in the apartment building's tomb-like cellar. Soon it would be time to shake off the earth once more and take the pots inside. But because she wanted to forestall the day when the plant's carmine splash would yield to November's brown monochrome, she delayed the uprooting for as long as she dared. She swept around the pot collecting its detritus in a dustpan.

She had lived in the flat five floors above the avenue for more than four decades. Today was the first day she had ever seen a workman in a mechanical extension bucket manipulating wooden poles to create a scaffold against the building opposite. She counted six. She leaned her head over her balcony's railing and measured with her eyes, calculating it would take another ten or eleven poles to reach the height of her geraniums. She wondered when that would be and if she would finally have quiet.

Pausing, she leaned against the railing and looked down across the broad avenue, a scene that had changed only in small ways through the decades. Her attention settled on a bistro, *La Brertagne* was tucked along side of the three-hundred steps leading downward from the R E R stop. Its name was painted in sky-blue cursive on a taupe, half-furled awning, Until three or four years before, perhaps five, it was called *La Vie en Rose,* when a famous chanteuse stopped to use the phone at the bar and the opportunistic owner took a photo and edited himself, taken on a separate occasion, onto her image, so it appeared they were sitting side-by-side. The rendering and reproduction of the photo into a full-blown photomural — plus a twenty-five percent increase in prices — served to rescue the bistro's owner from then-impending bankruptcy. She recalled that earlier the bistro had been named a variant of *"la tour Eiffel"* because, by standing on one of the sidewalk café tables next to the stairs leading to the R E R stop, one could see a reflection of the utmost tip of that symbol of Paris. Before, in times gone by, the bistro bore another name, so many names and so long ago, now beyond recall!

Today the tables were vacant, save one where a young man sat. She believed she had seen him sitting there another time.

Her attention shifted to the stationery and news shop once owned by a Monsieur Ravenelle and his wife. It had been, she recalled, Monsieur Ravenelle's custom to arrive at work shortly after the bistro opened. Tugging two revolving display-trees of postcards to the sidewalk outside his shop he would then trot to the bistro to order a *coffee-grande,* carry it back to sit, taking in the passing scene and sip his drink 'till his first customer arrived. His wife would arrive about an hour later, tugged along by two tandem-leashed poodles. Madame was known to exchange pleasantries with patrons and to throw lobs at politicians and other targets of opportunity. When she could find no customers inclined to listen, she would sit and flip through the latest *Paris Match,* folding over corners of the pages that interested her.

Both Monsieur and Madame Ravenelle took turns watering the four small geranium plants that strained for light from holders at the bottom of their shop's window. Sometimes when the old woman would go to the shop, she would find it attended by a young medical student. His name, *Jules,* was embroidered on his scrub shirt. Once when he served her, she had noticed he had delicate hands and was probably training to be a surgeon. Jules, she learned, had come to Paris from a coastal town in Brittany and was now living with a friend of an aunt in Paris.

One day when she went to the stationery shop for a newspaper, she found a black funeral wreath hanging on its locked door. When she returned the next day and the day after, she found the door still locked. For almost two weeks, she took her watering pot across the street and tended the four geraniums, but she soon gave up hope as well as her visits and the flowers died.

Her reverie about the Ravenelles dissolved as her attention again focused on the young man sitting at a *la Bretagne* table. Now she recalled him He was alone, alert and curious, at the same table a week or so before. But even his good looks couldn't keep her gaze from moving up the hundred or more steps to the R E R commuter halt. A blue-and-white train carrying passengers from *la Défense* to Versailles had just slowed to a stop and its riders were disembarking onto the platform. The scene reminded her that Irene, her young "niece," would be coming by in a week on her way to what she claimed was her ballet class. She knew that Irene, at thirty-one, was too old to take ballet, but she said nothing because any companionship at all was better than none.

The two had met by chance at a dining terrace atop one of Paris' favored department stores, *Prentemps...*

The waiter came forward with a silver tray, its napkin enfolding a note.

"A telephone message, Madame, just now!"

"Merci."

She scanned the note, telling of her old friend's unavoidable detainment elsewhere and slipped the note into her purse.

Madame de la Roche, who was actually believed to be a famous Countess of certain reputation among theatre folk was musing what to do about lunch: take it solitarily (not very enjoyable, that) when she noticed a very well dressed young lady with a baby in a pram, awaiting a table. Always gregarious, Madame had instructed a waiter to invite her to join and this, Irene Gaspard did.

The friendship caught, especially since Irene was wearing an engagement ring that had been given her in betrothal and, sad memories aside, practicality had taken over and she had decided that she would keep it.

The sapphire was large. Antoine had inherited it from an aunt and it was the aunt's and Madame de la Roche's birthstone, as well.

"I had earrings with that stone, my dear; when I was in the theatre, one of my dearest friends, Mistinguett had gotten them from a Count-you do remember Mistinguett, don't you? She was most famous even before the First World War, no, silly me. I keep forgetting I'm getting older—"

"But I have heard of her, of course," Irene demurred as the old lady lapsed back into what was basically a monologue of her entire life.

"—time does creep, then leap ahead and one day you're looking back and asking, 'where did it go, I was having so much fun!'; Her real name was Jeanne Bourgeois and she started by singing on the street, selling flowers. She introduced 'Mon Homme', The American, Fanny Brice made it famous as 'My Man'; let's see, I do go on, don't I? "Anyway, the Count was penniless but with a grand Chateau, near the gorge in Morlaix, but Mistinguett's career was beginning to burst out and he got nasty about it all and months later at the dressing table-we were doing some frothy thing at the Moulin Rouge-she turned to me and said,

'Every time I put these on, I think of him. I don't want to think of him. Here, you take them. They will match your eyes.'

"And she did, and they still do! And it was that simple. Then she went on to become more famous and I, less so. Then I married! And, look we've been here for two hours, I can't believe it! I'll bet your husband will be expecting you home?"

"Actually, my husband and I..."

"Oh, my dear," she said, deliberately contriving the wrong conclusion, "I'm so sorry. I didn't mean... to... pry."

But she did and both, being women of instinct, knew it, but both let it pass. She arose and so did Irene and Madame de la Roche slipped her an engraved card and the two bussed and that was the way the long friendship had begun, more than six years before.

*   *   *

Today her thoughts roved as she stood on her balcony, peering down at the traffic. The intersection was filled with automobiles and motorbikes, hungry for space, sometimes not their own and she would occasionally hear a collision. Sometimes the drivers would exit their cars and exchange politeness or sometimes, profanities. At other times, an ambulance would arrive. Now she watched as an old man was being pushed in a wheel chair. One day she might not be able to move about and would have to be pushed in a chair, like poor Madam LeFevbre with whom she had attended gymnasium between the wars and looked so much like her that they would dress alike and flirt with the same men. But when poor Madame LeFevbre went too far with a British officer and had to go out to *Provence* to have the child, their girlhood ended; and to think, Madam LeFevbre now lived in the apartment just under her own, alone and unassisted, that is, until the previous week when she took on a woman to help her about. She had lent Madam LeFevbre a wheel chair she had once needed when she had broken a leg and needed one to get about. Now, the two old ladies were the only tenants remaining in the building. This made her uneasy. Especially since she had received *the letter.*

The letter revealed that the building, so old that no one knew the exact year it was built, was in need of expensive repairs and that, before these repairs were undertaken, the remaining tenants might wish to avail themselves of a generous cash payment and vacate their apartments. To remain, the letter advised, might be dangerous. She had put the letter away, intending to talk to her "niece" about it, but whenever Irene arrived, the letter was forgotten.

She clipped three geranium blossoms and shuffled indoors to look for a container. She settled on a small glass vase with yellow and red enamel dots, pausing, remembering the day she received it: a Sunday afternoon, much the same as this one, but long before she had met her husband. It was, in fact, several lovers before him. As she set down her arrangement on the kitchen table, a bee that had curled up inside a withered leaf to die, tumbled out onto the table. She picked it up and carried it to her sink.

She was unaware that across the street at the *la Bretagne* table, the alert young man had not taken is eyes off of her as she had moved about. He set his coffee cup onto his saucer, still not taking his eyes from her balcony. He drummed his fingers on the table and pondered. *There has to be a way. Some way. Any way. But some way.*

*   *   *

Chapter 26

Paris, avenue Salengre, a fall day in nineteen-eighty

Vivian de la Roche, the woman Irene refers to as "aunt", reflected on how the stairs of her apartment building had been hollowed by thousands of boots, shoes, clogs and, once, eons before, hooves of the Percheron mount of a royal blood on an escapading up the stairs with two willing maiden captives. This afternoon, the steps still sweated moisture from the previous night's chill. She wanted to avoid falling, so she clung cautiously to the handrail until she had reached the worn stones of the ground floor.

Across the foyer, she tugged open the pedestrian entrance of the carriage door and blinked at the sudden sunlight of the street. Ducking under a construction pole, she reached the curb and waited for the semaphore to change to green before crossing to the *brassier Bretagne*. She passed under its fluttering awning and by three tables of customers sipping coffee, chatting, or reading. She hoped her slow ascent up the steps to the commuter railroad would not result in her missing the next blue-and-white car to *La Defense*. In fact, she was in time to make the first car and, in turn, her métro line *La Defense* connection that would carry her to a narrow street in the nineteenth *arrondissement*.

The car was nearly full, so she pulled down one of the folding seats directly by the entrance. As she waited for the door to close, she listened to mechanical ticking noises mingling with murmured conversations. Tobacco stench reeked from a large workingman on the fold-down seat next to hers. The warning horn blared, and the door began sliding closed. She saw a young man reaching the end of the station escalator, his arms filled with several packages that he juggled as he sprinted toward the train. He was but inches from the door when it closed and the train moved off. She saw that he was angry, his head jerking to one side, his mouth turning downward in defeated exasperation.

As the train passed swiftly into the *Métropolitan* underground system, she pulled open her purse and took out a small piece of paper on which she had written directions. The writing proved too small to decipher under the train's interior lights, so she rummaged in her purse until she found a small magnifying glass. With the help of the glass, she studied the paper till she was satisfied that she knew what she was about and, casting a look around as if to ward off any would-be thieves, she stuffed the glass and her paper back into her purse, snapped shut the lid, and clasped the bundle to her bosom.

A short while later, the train pulled to a halt at *les Grand Boulevards*. She urged herself up the *correspondence* stairway leading from her train, pulling herself up by the wall railing, trying not to slow the stream of passengers exiting into the white-tiled hallway and not blocking those climbing the stairs to the boulevard. On the street itself, lights on a cinema marquee danced for her attention, but she was concerned to find a blue-and-white enamel street sign on the corner of the nearest building's first floor. Once found, she searched out the building's entrance, an unkempt doorway and a bank of call bells for six apartments. Beside each bell an oblong brass frame identified the occupants, their names printed in neat script or erratic scrawl. One was labeled "B. Tangalese, *voyeur les avenirs — les anciens.*" She pushed the bell. A buzzer sounded. She opened the unlocked door and trudged up the ancient stairway.

A genial, smiling woman led her into an ornately furnished room with velvet curtains drawn against the late afternoon sun.

"Please, sit, and have some tea. You must be exhausted from the journey."

She was glad for the tea. She sipped at it till it was quite gone, then turned and looked questioningly at the medium — for that is what the turbaned mulatto was.

"I want you to tell me what he wants."

The medium fingered her large bejeweled necklace and fixed her gaze upward, slightly above her visitor's head, trying to recall what the lady, known to her as *"Comtesse,"* had imparted on the telephone some days earlier.

"Of course. That is understandable." Her eyes closed. She slumped.

Madame Tangalese leaned forward. A mirrored globe descended from within the drapery covering the ceiling, a point several inches above the polished inlaid table. She gazed into her own reflection.

"He has been departed for ... it's cloudy...some years."

"Over fifty."

"I see a uniform. He wears it. And I hear noises, explosions, but they do not seem to cause him fear. I see a long box. He is fearful for you. Are you hearing noises at night, *Comtesse?*"

"Yes."

"Has he spoken to you?"

"Sometimes I think he may have tried. When I call out his name, I hear a thumping noise and some music, that is, almost music...but not quite. It's always late at night. It goes for a while, the thumping and the other weird sounds, and then it's quiet."

"Let's sit for a moment and see if he will come near. You have to concentrate, because the departed always want to communicate, but we don't always let them back into our lives. Now, you mustn't be frightened by these visits. Are you frightened by them? No? Good. Here. Take my hands in yours."

*   *   *

Paris, Montparnasse metro, two hours before

Melville Saint-Eustace, his arms filled with stacked packages and his briefcase, elbowed his way out of the Galleries Lafayette and into the entrance of the nearby metro. He had tried to beat the late Friday afternoon rush hour, but the summer crowds, even in *Montparnasse,* had already begun their weekend exodus from the city to the coast and to the mountains. At his transfer station, he wished he had left some of his parcels behind. The balancing act slowed his progress through the *correspondence* hallway and up the stairs to the connecting platform for the Number One line. His heart sank when he heard the warning siren announcing the closing of his train's doors. He paced irritably as he watched the train pull away. It would be another seven minutes before the next one appeared.

He still had eight more stops and then a three-block dash down *rue Saint-Dominique* to the shop that closed at six-o'clock. It was already five-forty. His anxiety had peaked at boarding the *Métro,* having weighed its expense against his modest income but knowing absolutely that the gold locket was right, exactly right, the perfect gift for the girl who had started working at his flower shop a month before.

And in Sarah Goldschmidt's shop, at that very moment, another young man rested his elbows on the counter, settled his chin in his palms and watched Sarah examine a ring.

"How much?" he asked, urgently.

When she finished examining the ring through her jeweler's glass, she set the stone on the counter. Hesitantly, she asked, "What do you think it is worth, Antoine?"

"A thousand francs. Maybe twelve-hundred?"

"That's absurd. Here, take it back. Give it to someone. It'll make a nice keepsake." She shoved the ring toward him. "Well, please, Madame Goldschmidt, can you give me three hundred for it?"

"Two-fifty; that's generous. Take it or—"

A plaster frog sentry at the door croaked as a neatly dressed young man pushed through the door, breathing heavily.

Antoine clutched the ring in his fist and withdrew to an adjacent counter.

"That locket in the window, the gold one, how much is it?"

Sarah stated a price.

"Can I do payments, say, for six months?"

"It's possible. I must do a form first. Basic stuff. I can see you have great affection for the locket, so I'm sure that whomever you are buying it for will also like it very much. How much do you want to pay on it today?"

A sum was agreed upon. Sarah asked, "What name should I put on the receipt?"

"Daumier. Vernon Daumier."

The young man declined the offer to have it wrapped. Instead, he put it in his pocket and turned toward the door. The clay sentry croaked again. As he opened the door, he spoke over his shoulder, "Your frog needs singing lessons. *Au revoir,* Madame". Vernon Daumier hastened out of the shop and along the sidewalk. Within a few paces he had brushed against of another young man hurrying oppositely with an armload of packages. One of the packages fell. With mumbled apologies, Vernon stooped to help retrieve the box. Two more boxes fell in the confusion. When Melville stood up with all three packages, he was startled to recognize a friend from university days when they had worked at Vernon's family newspaper.

"Vernon?"

"Melville. How are you? Here, you are carrying too many things."

"Yes. Fine. Fine. How is your father, still looking for lost semi-colons?"

The two exchanged phone numbers and were again on their separate ways, Vernon crossing the boulevard. At its end, he took the adjoining avenue with sidewalks so narrow they did not allow two pedestrians abreast. He adjusted the earpiece of his Walkman and turned up the volume. Felice Joulliard was singing *"J'attendrai."* Taking the locket from his jacket pocket and examining it as he walked, he was trying to open it when his toe caught a loose cobblestone and he fell headlong into the path of a rushing *Citréon*. As his suddenly-still body lay in the gutter, his face turned ashen, and blood trickled from his mouth and ears, the locket clutched in his grasp.

Melville Saint-Eustace sighed in displeasure as he came upon the shop. The *Ferme* sign hung in the door. Final. No reprieve. He looked at his watch: nine past six. He looked in the window for the locket. It was gone. *"Merde!"* he thought in exasperation, "Someone else had all the luck."

He turned about and headed toward *Pont Neuf* with his packages, wondering if the absence of the locket was a sign. Maybe she wasn't the right girl, after all.

*   *   *

Chapter 27

A small shop on the rue de Omer Talon, Paris, the nineteen-eighties

Irene climbed the last few steps leading from the *Saint-Ambrose* metro station on *Voltaire* and paused momentarily, checking her bearings, looking about. Her last trip here was so far back she couldn't remember. Did she even remember the street? The locale collaged in her mind. She had the address on a slip of paper that she pulled from her purse; then, seeing a building of believed recall, in the middle of the block, she strode forward. Passing several intersections, she paused at each one, glancing down the narrow streets and alleyways, looking upward to the first floor of each corner building for the blue enameled street name. Finally she came to one, she believed was the one stuck in her memory; *rue de Omar Talon, a sens unique.* That it was a one way and she had sometime before walked against the opposing traffic strobed her memory, regaining her certainty. She recalled the unkempt shop, one of dozens in the wholesale district of the city, as being at the far end of a block, but today she came upon it suddenly, only four shops from *Voltaire.*

She pushed open the shop's glass door. A small alarm cat, sitting on plaster haunches, approximated a meow as Irene's feet broke its electronic beam. The shopkeeper was not about, though thuds and scrapings from a back room indicated that she was not to be alone for long. She passed her eyes over the shelves cluttered with figurines, placemats, and a dinner set advertised for sixteen—francs-fifty, now at twelve francs-forty with four salad plates and two chipped coffee cups.

Irene shifted her attention to a few paces beyond, a faux-feathered parrot, with one foot broken off, lay on its side in a rust-spotted cage.

Suddenly, his approach silent, he loomed behind her.

"Mademoiselle?"

"I need something for a screen, a decorative room screen. I was thinking of some prints, something with wild animals or flowers?"

He turned and beckoned her to follow. "In this corner, there are some boxes of prints. They are all priced reasonably. Don't look for any original *Degas* or *Lautrec*. This box, here, and this one, too, might do. Also, I have some in folders, which are larger. You can look, and if you find something, I will be over at the counter ready to assist you."

"Thanks," she responded as she leaned toward the boxes to start her search. Twenty minutes went by. Nothing had drawn her in. She moved a box aside to gain access to another. In it, besides yellowed magazine clippings, was a carton of photographs, black-and-white, ten-by-twelve centimeters.

"Interesting," she murmured aloud.

The photos included enlarged coastal scenes, biology slides, parallel specimen shots, and views through a microscope. A family sitting at a formal dining table, dressed for the best the 1915's had to offer. The father in severe high collar, the mother to his right, extending her arm across the table to touch his hand, two boys suited store window perfect, sitting side by side, a shoulder haired girl in dirndl; opposite them, a servant at the back, arms folded. Where were they now? The father under a white cross at the great cemetery of *Verdun*? The two boys dead on the battlefield at the *Somme*? The girl, fat and maternal and possibly dead? Who took the picture? Impossible for them to realize in that in that precious moment past that a complete stranger would be asking invasive questions. Irene's musing, invaded by time constraints, pulled several sea shore prints and headed for the counter.

"I think I have found what I want. How much for these?"

"For you — since these were taken by none other than our own Louis Pasteur twenty years before the invention of photography and because I want them to have a good home — ten francs each or, let me see..." He proceeded to count the pictures.

"Actually, if I remember these correctly, a medical student brought these in some time ago. Some are quite good." He named a sum.

She reached into her small purse and paid. On her way out the door, she paused. "You were quite right about the *Degases* and *Lautrecs*. There weren't any. *Au revoir*, Monsieur."

A short while later, Irene let herself into the *Gallerie LaGrande* and went to her desk. She turned on the light and spread the photos before her. The scenes she gravitated toward were not the specimen shots, but the seascapes, including several segments that featured local inhabitants and tourists, presenting a kind of travel guide to numerous coastal harbors. She was startled to find one that portrayed the light from a storm cloud above the bay at *Roscoff*. It must have been taken from her parent's hotel. How could that be? And by whom? The harbor wall, the low tide, the wooden boats resting casually on their sides, took her back in time, momentarily. Another view featured a neighboring port, but she could not place any of the others. One photo segment captured a little boy clad in a sailor shirt being led up a stone stairway typical of the Brittany coast. Suddenly, it came to her. The little boy's shirt would match the style of the new Chanels for Madame LaGrande's opening. She would enlarge the child to life-size. Mounted on hardboard, there would be several images of the boy on display. Madame would be pleased, and might even decide at last to agree to Irene's request for a raise.

She placed her magnifying glass against the photo to check for defects. As she did so, her attention turned to the adult leading the little boy up the stairs. The man's face looked strangely familiar — probably the typical French tourist face from the era. The clock chimed the hour, interrupting her thoughts.

"God, I'll be late. Vernon promised me a birthday present. The locket, perhaps?" She turned out the desk light and hurried out into the dusk.

*   *   *

Arriving at her apartment, Irene climbed the six flights to her apartment and fitted the key into the lock. The lack of heat in the flat demanded she turn on the electric heater. She inserted a *cinque-franc* coin into the heater and lit the oven to warm two slices of quiche. The water in the shower ran cold, ice cold, so she leaned away from the stream while she fiddled with the faucet handle. She was all goose bumps as she slipped into a pale blue blouse—Vernon's favorite because of its sheer material. Unfortunately, it provided no warmth, especially since Vernon preferred that she wear it without a slip or bra. Finished dressing, she went over to the dormer windows that peaked from the mansard roof to the narrow, rainy street below. She wanted to catch a glimpse of Vernon as he rounded the corner almost directly below. Vernon always looked up and threw her a kiss that she would catch and hold to her breast.

Perhaps it was still too early. She reached for the phonograph and clicked its start switch. *"J'attendrai"* dipped and swelled. It was their song, and Vernon's favorite. The rain continued to fall as she stood in the recess of the dormer, waiting for Vernon's kiss. But tonight there would be no kiss, not tonight, nor any other night, ever again. The ambulance's siren and the sound of its tires sluicing through the rain-drenched streets preceded its flashing blue light. Inside, the ambulance attendant tenderly took the locket from Vernon's grip and then adjusted the coverlet over his pallid face.

*   *   *

Chapter 28

Paris, hospital Val De Grace, later that night

The ambulance, its speed slowed for the previous ten minutes of its trip, its emergency light off, turned left off *Boulevard Port de Royal,* into the small alleyway and backed up to the emergency entrance.

Jules Gaspard watched the two attendants pull the litter out of the vehicle, its legs unfolding to support its sad burden and watched the two labor it through the door. He wiped the interior of the ambulance with a cloth soaked in disinfectant. He thought he had taken care of everything, but, as he checked the supplies, he found that a spare blanket had been spattered with blood. He reflected how the blood, already dried to umber, had but a short while before coursed through the veins of a young man his own age, had provided force for his heart, had been excited in love, and, now, had been mingled with the wool fibers of a sheep like the ones that he had watched graze in the fields of Brittany when he was still a boy. He wadded up the blanket together with his cleaning cloths and a cleaning brush, tossing them into a wheeled basket.

After inspecting his work, he gathered some loose objects, a back pack, a pocket knife, a *deux-franc* coin, a *cinq franc* coin, some *centiémes,* a Métro ticket, a rabbit foot key chain, a cinema stub, *"de Sang Froid"*-how entirely, mordantly appropriate, "detritus of death"-had they fallen from his pocket onto the street? If so, how did they get to the ambulance floor? Stepping down from the cabin, he closed the ambulance door. He wheeled the soiled materials down the glaring white porcelain floor tiles of the hospital corridor until he reached a laundry chute. He opened the hatch and pitched in the blend of human blood and sheep fiber, a weave that he wouldn't see again till it had been cleansed of its current morbidity. He continued down the hall to a security window. Its plain glass, he noted, had probably not been cleaned since it had been inserted into a wood frame when a hospital had been created from a nineteenth-century convent a hundred years before. On the other side of the smudged window, an older man with a gray, untrimmed moustache sat angled to the glass, reading *La Temps*.

Jules rapped on the window. The man let his newspaper fall and turned on his swivel chair. He leaned forward to reach the window, which he swung in and hooked to a chain dangling from above.

"*'Soir.*"

"*Bonne soir,* I've just finished a run. The emergency crew left me to clean up. I have some valuables to turn in."

He pulled a clipboard from a shelf and shoved it toward Jules and fingered spaces on the form.

"Patient's name and address and a list of the stuff."

"Deceased."

"Then, you put in the name and all the data anyway and check 'deceased' in the box on the top line. Put the items in here." He retrieved a brown envelope.

Jules toiled industriously with a billfold, its zipper not working properly, containing the victim's name, and a slip of paper with an address, some smaller value coins and, finally, a gold locket.

"Was he wearing that?" the gray moustache asked.

"No. Just holding it. He was hit by a car."

"Oh. You sign here." He fingered a line.

Jules wrote his name and asked, "Is that all?"

"Yes. That's all. The morgue will take it from here."

The moustache released the window from its chain and closed it, murmuring, "*Au revoir, Monsieur le Docteur Gaspard.*"

Jules, surprised, but pleased to be taken for a certified doctor, replied, "*Au revoir. Merci, Monsieur.*" As he walked away, he thought about the clenched hand of the deceased and the locket it once held so tightly.

*   *   *

Roscoff, l'Auberge Gaspard, the same evening

At the same instant, in Roscoff, Catherine Gaspard stood in her nightdress at the window, watching the surf pound the moonlit harbor. The small sailboats bounced recklessly on the carpeting surf. As she looked out, she thought she could see little Jean-Baptiste standing on the seawall with a haunted, wondering expression on his face. She involuntarily raised her hand as though to wave.

*   *   *

Chapter 29

Paris, Le Gallerie LaGrande, the next day

The next morning, Irene, still smarting from Vernon's neglect from the night before, her concentration distracted from a final organization of the sets for the fashion-show fundraiser. Not only he hadn't shown up at her apartment, but worse, he hadn't called! Cold fury smoldered within her. She would tell Vernon a thing or two. This wasn't the first time. She hated to think it was coming to an end, but enough is *enough*. Four artisans gathered near her, awaiting instructions. A quarter hour later, she explained her scheme for a photomontage to be added to the already completed seascape. She needed to create a seaside resort town ambience, in front of which would be several cutout figures, more than life-size, mounted on thick paper-board. She related the dimensions of the stage at the prestigious hotel off the Trocadero where the tableaux would be installed as a backdrop to a fashion walk.

A telephone rang from another part of the room.

"Irene, it's Madame LaGrande. She needs to talk!"

Irene took the phone.

"Madame? Yes, of course, I understand. I'll arrange everything. The hotel is taking care of the additional flowers. And Alain Bernard has agreed to play piano, after all. Now, do you know, was the truck ordered for the transport? Thanks, Madame. No, I have two days off from Bernard Foucard. I'm all yours. I'll see you at the hotel tomorrow, then. Will you be coming directly from Orly? Okay. Fine."

She used the same phone to order the photo enlargements. She insisted that the company would have no choice but to have them ready in twenty-four hours.

*   *   *

The following day, Irene supervised the laying out of the set at the hotel. The harbor background mural with its undulating lighting effects emulated the sweeping grays of the sea. Several faux-granite rocks framed the scene. When the images of the little boy in the sailor shirt finally arrived, she had them mounted on their stands and placed where the models of the summer collection would easily be able to avoid them on their perambulations.

All too rapidly, time collapsed and the evening was upon her. While guests swathed in Italian silks swished, Chanels pirouetted, and pointed toes balleted; the seaside motif put the patrons in a jaunty mood. Servers mingled with trays of canapés and flutes of *Möet*. The room overflowed with poses, meaningful gestures, some sincere, others not, superficialities and cryptic looks, stolen glances askance. Subdued recordings of the Atlantic surf insinuated through murmured conversations. The attar of rose bouquets competed with wafting scents of *Channel* and *Guerlain*.

A half hour passed. And another hour; Joline LaGrande had yet to appear. Finally, a murmur of appreciation washed through the room when she did arrive. Her flight had been delayed and she was still attired in her travel pantsuit. She waltzed into a corner of the room, bussing here, embracing there, and then retired to change. A quarter of an hour later, she reappeared in a wine-colored sequined sheath with matching pumps and a simple gold necklace. When she spotted the major guest of the evening, a seigniorial sculptor glancing about for her, she made a rapid pass through the crowd in his direction. Complementing the recorded sounds of the surf, the pianist Alain Bernard ambulated traditional tunes as Jean-Baptiste stood nearby, his gaze shifting between Alain and the photomontage. Alain, again at a loss and pretending nonchalance, was transfixed by Jean-Baptiste. What had begun some weeks before with a mere touch on his shoulder in Le Piano Zinc now consumed him. He argued with himself that it had been like this a dozen times before. But the youth from the provinces dominated his every thought. He knew he needed total possession, for even a night, if he were ever to feel total release.

Joline LaGrande, meanwhile, was introducing sculptor Renault Pampour-Ampersand, whom the guests knew by reputation if not by sight. His most recent excursion into notoriety had been the shooting a cable from a tower of *Notre Dame* to the *Hotel de Ville* in the middle of one night. The next morning, giant multi-colored plaster of Paris phallic and testicular forms swung from the cable as if floating in the air. Pampour-Ampersand was arrested and quite quickly released, to the vast amusement of the press and the somewhat more subdued amusement of church officials. Tonight, bearded and attired in a denim, lime-colored jacket with a red chiffon scarf about his neck, he linked arms with a newly-introduced guest, a woman ten kilos too heavy and three sizes too big for her turquoise sheath dress. From her wrists a mélange of etched and enameled brass jangled in a barbarous cacophony that bespoke renunciation of minimalist stylistic decorum. The sculptor's free arm waved expansively while declaiming, "The density and textures of rejuvenating, anthropomorphic tendencies and the reformed realities of form and function have a centurion effect on the human reactionary space." A polite patter of applause encouraged him.

Joline LaGrande was not as captivated. She handed her half-empty flute to a waiter and familiarly grasped the bare arm of a similarly skeptical guest.

"I have been looking for you. I've seen a fabulous Henry Moore that I know needs a new home. Very reasonable, under the circumstances — that is, reasonable for a Henry Moore. Perhaps I can put out a feeler for you?"

"I trust your judgment, Joline. My husband says that you are the best in Paris, perhaps even in New York, and if you think it is reasonable —" The patron stopped in mid-sentence. She watched as Joline's face drained to a colorless vacancy as her eyes fixated on the photomural on the nearby wall.

Joline withdrew her hand from the patron's arm and murmured, "Pardon." Slowly, she stalked to the photo tableaux and stared, and turned about. She examined the cardboard mounted little boy in the sailor shirt, as tall as she, before striding up to the grainy harbor view and standing within mere centimeters of the mural. She focused her eyes on two figures on a flight of stone steps. Staring, her arms akimbo on her hips, then dropping and, once again traveling to her hips, then, once more dropping and finally she placed one arm against her chest, fingering her necklace, her other hand under her chin before stiffening and turning, lips taut, beckoning Irene from the crowd, to her side. With a look of withering perplexity, she tapped her fingers against the images and hissed,

"How could you do this... this, Irene? How could you do ... *this?*" She spun about and stalked from the room, the sequins on her *merlot* dress flashing her fury.

*   *   *

Irene returned to the hotel the next morning, supervising the workers she had engaged to disassemble the photomural. She studied its pieces, searching for a clue to help understand Joline's high dudgeon over the display. She blamed herself for assuming that her employer would enjoy seeing *Roscoff* and its wooden boats as backdrop to a Parisian fete. Perhaps it was Joline's memories of the village instead of the photos which had caused such a severe reaction. Her eyes explored the largest segment of the scene, revealing the middle of the harbor's crescent, between the lighthouse and the seawall. At once, two figures appeared that, on the small original image, had not been apparent. One of the figures was a boy in a sailor shirt — the source of the enlarged portrait she had not thought to associate with the larger harbor view. A man in a worker's jumpsuit, looking directly up at the camera, was leading the way for the child. Irene stepped back, trying to find the best distance from the enlargement to gauge the details of the man's face. Even though the photograph had been taken at some remove, the features of the adult figure were quite clear: the wide-set eyes, the rounded chin, determined set of the mouth — a familiar face. Irene tensed as a memory of that face erupted from her past at *Gallerie LaGrande*. A party. That face had arisen from a modish tuxedo at one of Joline's soirées and was *not* the face of a man, but, rather, unmistakably, that of Joline LaGrande herself.

*   *   *

Chapter 30

Paris, a funeral chapel, two days later

Melville Saint-Eustace studied the part in her hair and the nape of her neck. Because he was seated directly behind her and because it had been so long since he had seen her, he wasn't sure it was she. It had been years since he had lived in *Roscoff,* where his parents now lay buried and where his aunt once ran the flower shop and where he had once played with the Gaspard children. To think they were now mourning their mutual friend. He leaned forward and whispered, "Irene?"

Irene had been staring numbly at the casket and was startled to hear her name. She twisted around to see who was speaking. "Melville?" She hesitated, groping for his last name, "Melville Saint-Eustace?"

He touched her shoulder. "Yes. Certainly. I'm so sorry..." he whispered.

"Thank you for coming."

"We can talk after the ceremony."

"Thank you, Melville, so kind of you." Irene returned to her meditation on the casket. Soon, her head bowed as she unconsciously kneaded one hand with the other. Occasionally, she glanced over at Vernon's parents who sat closer to their dead son. She barely knew them. In fact, they had met only once, and they had not approved of her. The decisions for the funeral had been theirs to make. Now, as the chapel organ pumped out a canned number, Vernon's father, mute and cragged as a *Brittany* cliff, appeared truly grief-struck. His bureaucratic moustache, reminiscent of some *belle-époque* cartoon, occasionally trembled. He seemed cowed, but then he had seemed so to Irene on their only meeting when he had just lost his newspaper business and was facing even more years of marriage and the care of six children still at home. The mother fidgeted with a rosary as if counting the betrayals of the rhythm system and the burden of the day's events — yet another nail in the cross of her martyrdom. Five of Vernon's siblings, some with partners, filled the front stalls of the chapel.

Irene realized she could never share with any of them what she knew of Vernon, and not only their intimacies, but also the instances of their shared confidences. He would have hated the open casket and being made to hold a rosary. Whose idea was that? His mother's no doubt. Vernon would have flung the thing away and laughed. Vernon's laughter was what first drew her to him. She had been at the beach with friends when he had squealed up on his motorbike, sprayed them with dirty wet sand and laughed. And he laughed on their long walk in the wooded park near the *Loire* and again after they had given in to one another. He had even laughed when she insisted on her interest in the locket in the shop window. Maybe if she had not been so insistent. But that was always her way, insistence leading to disaster. How could she explain this impulse for uncontrolled wanting? She couldn't explain her impulses, not to herself at anytime and certainly not here, now, with Vernon lying there as the very definition of mortuary pallor embedded in a stretch of pink quilting, the rosary in his hands and the parents and brothers and sisters at his side — all because of the locket. The damn locket, found clutched in his hand after the car struck him down on his way to her apartment.

With the service over and her good-byes silently rehearsed, she stood with the others on the chapel's stone steps. The casket was carried past her to the waiting hearse. The family made no attempt to invite her to the gravesite. She tilted her face up into the late afternoon mist. Melville approached from behind her.

"You look friendless. My moped is a block away. There's a new place up in *Montmartre*, the Dapper Owl, just off *rue Lepic*."

"Sure." She wasn't quite certain why she wanted to be with someone, except she knew she didn't want to go back to her attic apartment in the Fourth and its memories of Vernon, nor did she want to go alone to her usual upscale hangout in the Sixteenth. They walked a block down the narrow street to where Melville had left his dual-seat moped. He got on and cranked the engine and then handed her his helmet. She got on behind and donned the headgear. A moment later, they were whirring through rain-splashed cobbled streets.

When he reached the *Métro Blanche* near the Moulin Rouge, he swung up the steep cobbled ascent of *rue Lepic*. The bistro's insignia, a large owl wearing a derby hat, blinked an electric eye as they approached. Inside the Dapper Owl, a crowd of university types majoring in Marlboros occupied all but a single seat at the bar. Melville stood by Irene's side. She turned to him and spoke.

"Now, I remember. In *Roscoff* you didn't wear a helmet, either. I think that was the first time I saw you, riding the yellow Vespa, carrying a large lavender wreath down *Montaigne*."

"Good memory. Helmets are for idiots. Not that you're one. But I've always felt that I'm a careful biker."

They ordered aperitifs. An hour went by. When a couple left from a banquette, they took their place, Melville sliding in close to Irene's side.

She twisted her glass,

"When I got word about Vernon it seemed so pointlessly cruel. I mean, first he was here and then..." She turned away and put her forehead against her arm. She sobbed in barely audible bursts of whimpering, like a lamb nuzzling its mother.

Although none of the other patrons took notice, Melville was visibly shaken. He studied the skin of her neck as the neon eyes of the Dapper Owl painted it amber, then pink and then blue. Hesitantly, he reached for her shoulder to comfort her. As if expecting his touch, she turned her face to him and brushed her hair from her eyes. Then she gripped her drink and drained the glass. A moment later she cast her gaze on his mouth, reached out and touched him on the cheek.

"I mean, it was like being caught up in a giant accordion. First, he didn't show up, and then the damn flicks were there at my door with an envelope. All his stuff from the ambulance. With my address in his wallet. They didn't know I didn't know. *Et cette putain medallion!* I couldn't *stand* to look at it. And the next thing I knew it was today and he was in that awful box..."

She rested her head against Melville's shoulder. Her lashes glistened with tears, as she stared out into the street, seemingly uncomprehending as she dozed off. The neon eyes of the Dapper Owl flashed against her. Minutes passed, perhaps five or ten; Melville was becoming entranced by her closeness, the scent of her perfume. She awoke. Melville paid the tab and they walked out into the chilled dawn.

"I will take the metro from *Blanche,* Melville", Irene spoke as they mounted the motor bike. "I'm supposed to meet my aunt for breakfast and it just makes good sense to stay the night with her."

"Of course. Will I see you again, soon, I hope?"

"Certainement... mon Melville."

The motor bike glided through the alleys and thoroughfares until Melville brought it to a smart halt on *Salengre.* They bussed on the cheeks and her eyes followed him, as he sped away into the dawn, recalling the pause Irene had injected into her phrasing of *"mon Melville",* wondering if, in fact she was now claiming him for herself.

*   *   *

Chapter 31

Paris, Place de l'Opéra, the evening after the funeral

Melville lifted the azaleas from their sidewalk display stand and brought them into the shop. He put them on the floor against the flower cooler and then switched off the cooler's light. Back outside, he let down the shop's security lattice and locked it against night time intruders. A baguette vendor at the curb was also just closing for the night. Melville dashed to the food stand to grab the sole remaining *tomate-et-jambon* combination, which, once paid for, he nestled amongst the other items in his backpack. His moped waited for him against a nearby alley wall. As he unlocked it, he considered his route home. His usual journey to the shop each morning started at *Gare Nord* — close to where he lived and where he would pick up a small shipment of flowers just arrived from the Netherlands. He'd then travel directly along *rue Lafayette* to his shop near the opera. But, tonight, he would try a different route. He trotted alongside the scooter to start it and when the motor engaged, he hopped on and, in minutes, was weaving in and out of traffic along a vast conglomeration of boulevards that shingled onto one another — *Madeleine, Capucines, Italiens, Montmartre, Poissonniere.*

As he passed near *les Boulevards* and its *art neuveau* Métro halt, a light mist began to fall. He thought he might need his seldom-worn helmet, still tied to his moped's rear seat. He glanced back at it. Neon lights reiterated themselves in psychedelic splashes on the helmet's glossy finish. Just afterwards, while veering between a parked taxi and a lumbering bus, he was narrowly missed by a minivan edging to another lane. His new route, he decided, was turning out to be more exciting than he'd bargained for.

He wheeled onto *Bonne Nouvelle,* the boulevard, unique, he once noted, entitled for an abstraction and not for a famous field marshal or locale. At a sharp hairpin curve, he swung sharply up onto *rue de Lune,* a snake wending its way through a hodgepodge of narrow streets housing myriad, unkempt shops, (windows unwashed since the time of the Armistice in 1918?) of garment wholesalers. Finally, he pulled over at *12, rue de Thorel* and switched off his bike. He dismounted and locked up the vehicle, pleased, all in all, with his new route home.

As he went up the four flights of stairs to his rooms, he thought of the baguette in his backpack. It would be his reward for another completed workday. He ate it in the flickering cool halo of the television. Eventually, a banging pipe roused him from a stupor. It meant hot water was circulating. Throwing off his clothes, he showered, the first of the day, and luxuriated under needle-sharp splays of water pricking his back.

Once toweled off, he donned a robe and lay on the couch and tried to get some news out of a two-day-old *Le Monde,* but thoughts of Irene and *Roscoff* intruded. He compared his memory of her as a bright-eyed girl to how vacant-eyed she seemed after the funeral. He also recalled the turn of her head in the Dapper Owl as her grieving unfolded, interspersed with his memories of their early years on the coast.

He had told her about a box of letters and other effects he had been given after his aunt Fleur died in *Roscoff.* Irene had registered slight pique at his not sorting through them in a thorough way since he was a boy. He got up now and padded to his bedroom. From under his bed frame, he pulled out a shoebox, envelopes cornered with *Céres* postage stamps from the forties, covered with dust that had accumulated since his having moved into the garret nearly two years before.

He wiped away the dust with an old sock and placed the box on his duvet. Snapping on the bed lamp and he settled himself against a pillow. A clipping sailed to one side as he opened the box. A picture of a particularly gory automobile accident was captioned "Car Crash at *Rennes* Kills Local Merchant." The article mentioned a George and Monique Ravenelle, owners of a shop on avenue *Salengre,* near *Sevres.*

Melville put the clipping aside and took out some letters. They were old, from the 'forties, the war years. They were addressed to a Monsieur Renauld Penze in *Roscoff.* The *Céres* stamp was overlaid with a clumsily inked swastika and a postmark of Morlaix; its return mentioned only one "L. Vernet." A Nazi censor stamp bore harshly into the thin paper inside the envelope.

My dearest Klaus has been promoted. There are some interesting developments afoot about which I can't write to you now. Please write. Ever, Louise.

Melville thumbed through more of the letters. One, he noticed, was still sealed. Strangely, it bore no official censorial swastika stamp. His curiosity piqued, he slit the seal with his finger and pulled out a single sheet, dated October 30, 1942.

My dear Penze, This letter is being brought by a trusted friend. It's been almost three weeks since K.B. left for a short trip to Roscoff. Since he is valuable to us both and provides me lots of interesting news, this may explain why you have not heard from me. Any news you can transmit to me in care of the Bistro Riviera, 6 rue Rosignole, Fegreac, would be devoured instantly. Louise.

Melville sifted through the box until the early morning. As important as the papers might be for others, they meant less to him than the silver butter knife he found in the bottom of the box. It was from the set he used when he would bring croissants to his aunt on Saturday mornings in *Roscoff.* As for the letters, well, they might be of interest to an old school friend who now worked at the Foreign Ministry in *Paris.* He would send the letters to him.

*   *   *

Chapter 32

Paris, the Club Joline an evening, in the nineteen-eighties

Felice Jouiliard, a favorite for many seasons of the Parisian club scene, acknowledged the night's applause. She let her handheld microphone drop to her side and turned to speak to her piano accompanist. Then, as she faced the audience again, she lifted the mike and murmured, haltingly, in her husky trademark voice.

"This next song tells of another sort of love; a young woman who is waiting in her attic room for her lover to return. He's bringing her a gift. She stands at the window, wanting to catch a glimpse of him as he nears her building. She hears an ambulance siren and watches it's flashing blue light as it drives by. She doesn't know that it carries her lover, struck down by a car and nearing death. The song is called '*J'attendrai.*'"

Her accompanist, Alain, set the mood as he finessed the opening bars. Later, as Alain was changing out of his tuxedo, Felice knocked at his dressing room door.

"Alain, Alain. The publisher has sent over two new songs by courier. The box office didn't think they were important — those *aiguilliers* — so they didn't fucking get them to me, dear Alain, until five minutes ago. May I come in?"

"Of course, Mademoiselle Joulliard."

She pushed the door open and handed him the manuscripts.

"They look possible. Maybe if you like them I can get that *panier a crottes* to pay for them. By the way, her nephew, or whatever, was here last night and again tonight. Out front. Blonde. Very blonde. Your type, Alain?"

"Hardly, Mademoiselle. I like them five-two, no butts, and brunette. But thanks for the tip. How about if I look these over tonight? I'm due at *le Piano Zinc* for a late gig. I can run through them there."

"Fine. *Bonne nuit,* Alain."

"Bonne nuit, Mademoiselle."

From the hallway, Jean-Baptiste Gaspard, in search of his aunt's companion, had overheard the end of her conversation. He greeted Felice with adulations and begged his leave. His goal was *le Piano Zinc, a* few blocks away on rue *Blancs-Manteaux.* Jean-Baptiste was already sitting at a small table near the piano when Alain entered. He watched as the pianist ordered a *Perrier* from the bar and then propped a sheaf of music on the piano rack. He caught Alain's eye, but the pianist seemed to take no particular notice of him, which was far from the truth. Alain was suddenly fighting one of the most profound attractions of his life. He began to steal furtive glances at the young blonde. He fumbled at the keys. In an introduction to *"La Vie en Rose,"* he lost his train of thought. He started a new number, the theme from *Un Homme, Une Femme,* this time with success.

When Alain finished the set two hours later, he looked about the small room and saw the young man standing at the bar.

"Tall, turned up nose, not my type. So why am I going crazy?"

*   *   *

Saint-Saens' Number Four was soaring. Never had Alain felt such release at being used. It wasn't his usual role, and he was trying to claim some understanding of it and his unexpected attraction while wanting it to continue. They shifted. Jean-Baptiste lay still. Alain, aggressive, asked, "So, how'd it be if I do some artistry on le ballustrines? *Then, when you get bored with that, I can* faire une asperge."

A squeal of tires on the pavement outside his apartment woke Alain from his reverie. The morning sun streamed in. The scent of roasting coffee wafted in from the *brasserie* two floors below. Alain lay in bed, reluctant to allow the realities of the morning to erase the night's erotic imagery. He had left *le Piano Zinc* alone at two o'clock and had wrestled the night through with fantasies of Jean-Baptiste. Somehow, some way, he wanted to be a part of the young man's life.

*   *   *

Roscoff, the kitchen of Le Auberge Gaspard, the same morning

Catherine Gaspard had avoided looking at the lobby calendar all morning, but, eventually, she forced herself to change the date from 4 to 5 September. Jean-Baptiste's birthday was over. Though years had passed since the little boy had vanished without a trace, hardly a day had gone by that she had not looked out the kitchen window to the bay or out the foyer door to the garden court, expecting to see his five-year-old face. Even now, though thirteen birthdays had passed, she expected that he would enter the door looking the same as when he went away. It was only when she saw schoolchildren getting off the bus, and only then reality set in: her Jean-Baptiste was not going to get off the bus. Somewhere in *Lille, Besançon,* or *Paris,* he was a young man of eighteen.

Catherine still set a place for him at the supper table, hoping that he would come through the door and sit at his place and look expectantly at her as she took removed the casserole from the oven; he would cross himself after the blessing, as he had been taught. Etched in her mind was the image of the little red boat, tilted on the empty harbor floor, against the setting sun, and Jean-Baptiste's footprints leading away from it, forever. When such visions occurred after a meal, she would turn and lean against the sink and quietly sob, her body engulfed with grief.

*   *   *

Chapter 33

Paris, a commuter train, nineteen-eighties

The R E R commuter train gradually ascended the avocado-hued hill southwest of *Paris*. When it reached the *Sevres* station and came to a halt, Irene looked out, her gaze sweeping over the *Paris* skyline. To her left, the white dome of *Sacré-Coeur* stood gleaming atop *Montmartre*. To her far right, the fretwork of the Eiffel Tower stood at its ever-ready attention. Today, just after a shower, a rainbow pitched a muted arc over the scene, linking the two landmarks.

As the train hiccoughed to another start, her view shifted to the diorama of advertisements above the car's windows: a department store facade, a chocolate bar, the SCNF deluxe TGV to the Atlantic, and a map reminding her that the next stop, *Chaville,* would be hers.

She gathered her things and rose in anticipation. She had made the stop many times and now imagined how she would navigate her way through the small, three-sided glass shelter to the three-hundred steps leading down to the wide avenue *Salengre,* the main auto route between *Versailles* and *la Defense.*

Suddenly, the train slammed to an abrupt halt. Irene lurched forward and then recoiled back into her seat. Other passengers threw their arms out in front of them for support while their packages fell to the floor.

"Alors!"

"Merde!"

"Chose!"

"Imbéciles!" and other indignities flew through the air. Instant acerbic Gallic blame directed at the rail service, the stupidity of the bureaucracy murmured throughout the still wagons. Then, an expectant silence descended on the train's interior broken only by the striking of matches against match covers to re-light another *Galois*. Only slowly did random squeaks and the hissing of

pressure gauges begin to intermingle with subtle murmurs and sighs of the captive passengers. Minutes passed. The train remained stalled. More minutes went by — five became ten, then twenty, and thirty. More *Galois* lit. Moods shifted into a collective testiness. How much longer? Does anybody know anything? Why can't the idiots do any better? An hour passed before, finally, almost imperceptibly, the train began to creep to the *Chaville* stop — in fact, only meters away from the impromptu halt.

Irene jostled with others anxious to debark from the car. On the platform, they had to merge to a single file to avoid a mangled wheelchair propped against a barrier at the bottom of the stairs which Irene discovered for herself upon reaching g the last few steps. She slowed, then froze at the sight of the familiar crocheted shawl stretched across the chair's arms. Her thoughts flashed to her dear old friend, wondering what the future would hold. Images from the past shingle-invaded her mind, the reality of her disjointed life, the night at the supper table her mother's comment about her weight gain, and was it because she was pregnant, and her hushed reasoning-wholly impromptu and not protectively thought out-reply and her father's hands dropping to the table, fists forming, clenched Gothic jaw, mouth hissing hatred ordering her from their home, her flight by night train to *Paris,* the climb up the stairs of the attic five flights near rue *Lepic,* her chance meeting-fortuitous, that-with Bernard Foucard, her passion for Vernon, her shock at losing him, her growing affection for Melville, her little boy, Georges, now no longer little but a young man, almost the same age she was when Antoine abandoned her. But, now three hundred steps and half-way through her life-funny coincidence, that-she thought she was thinking positively. She was alive! Alive! Perhaps so well off that she might return to *Roscoff* and open a small restaurant with the liberal salary Bernard had given her along with expensive jewelry when their love affair was barely kindled those years ago, years that skipped forward in her mind as though they were but momentary flipping of pages in a book. And the comparison of her life and that of Madame de la Roche, now approaching the end of hers, she, Irene, still was vibrant and intellectually bright. And so was Madame de la Roche, even though she had adopted the persona of the stage beauty friend of hers who had died in the concentration camp those dreadful years in the Second World War. Irene remembered the shock of seeing the picture of Blanche Everon du Plais in the 1945 in *Les Temps,* emaciated, eyes bulging from sockets, clinging to the barbed wire, her death reported but days after the picture was taken.

How different the fortunes of the two ladies had been, both from small villages in *Provence*, both famous on the local stages, both with distressing marital ties but ones life torn asunder by the mania of war, and ending in a filthy barbed wire enclosure the other, through the fault of an errant newspaper printer, living comfortably, and most importantly, *living!*

Irene wondered-now she was at the last of the three hundred steps-how she, Irene could have dealt with the same problems.

At the curb, an attendant was closing the door on a municipal mortuary wagon. Though she quickened her pace, she could only watch the wagon speed off as she descended the last few steps to the ground.

She paused, waiting for the signal to turn. Impatient, she crossed against the red light and jogged to the entrance of the eighteenth-century building opposite. She noted that a new construction fence had been thrown up since she had last visited, and more than a dozen angled support poles had been set up against the brick walls. In juxtaposition to the curtains that still hung in her aunt's windows and in those of the old lady's apartment below, a contemporary sign proclaimed a new eminence, *Maison de Salengre*. The sign included a painted depiction of an ultra-contemporary, muted terra-cotta apartment building set back from the busy avenue. Below the rendering was the name of Bernard's firm painted in black, block cursive script.

Watching vacantly from a phone kiosk across the street was Bernard's new associate, Antoine. Antoine, who had little concern for what his boss's sometime secretary — and his old girlfriend, Irene — would find at the old lady's apartment, snapped to only when his call was connected. He couldn't disguise his smugness.

"You owe me 50,000 francs."

*   *   *

Vivian de la Roche opened her apartment door.

"I heard footsteps on the stairs and I knew it had to be you. You're late, but no matter."

"There was an accident. The train got held up. I think someone was killed. The train didn't move for an hour."

"How dreadful. Well, I'm glad to see you now. I'm feeling better today. Not like Madame LeFevbre on the floor below. She's had the grippe and has been chilled to the bone. I lent her my shawl. I think she gets cold sitting in that dreadful chair all the time. I know. I hated to sit in it all day after I twisted my hip. Isn't it funny how fate deals some of us better hands when it comes to aging and health?

"We were girls together, almost twins, but whereas she feels ninety, I feel forty. Well...perhaps closer to fifty. And I remember the Field Marshal's funeral in 'thirty-eight...no, 'thirty-nine, as if it were yesterday. Well, perhaps not like yesterday, but last week. Anyway, I have some good bread and some *pâté* and some wine. We can go out onto the balcony. Oh, I wish I had my shawl. Do you know, that dreadful woman who came to the door is now working for Madame LeFevbre? I wouldn't have a giant like that around me all the time. I saw she was trouble straight away. She's a goliath, three meters tall and 300 kilos if she's a gram. I don't know why the health department would have sent her in the first place. I sent her down to Madame LeFevbre because I knew I didn't need her. She barely spoke French. I had to *point.*"

Irene was too overwhelmed by the old woman's need to converse to tell her about the wheelchair at the station and her suspicions about the fate of Madame LeFevbre. Her underlying concern was her friend's entrancement with a pseudo identity, the adoption of the Field Marshall's widow's identity and the belief that she had become that person.

Further jamming these crashing complexities was her dread about the possibility of Bernard's involvement in so convenient, and perhaps fatal, accident.

"I'm famished," Irene hedged. "Perhaps I should stay the night: there was something I overheard at work today we can talk about in the morning. Something about your identity papers. Bernard is getting impatient and before he finds out who you really are, we should think about finding you a new place. But...tomorrow."

Irene lit a cigarette and sat at café table on the balcony while her friend turned away wordlessly. Presently she returned with an outlay of salads and puréed salmon on the table. Soon both were seated, eating with minimal conversation, taking in the Parisian sunset, sipping *a Beaujolais.* Dusk closed about the balcony and a wave of lights washed over the roofs of Paris. In the morning, Irene knocked on her aunt's door. There was no answer, so she went to the kitchen and started coffee. Presently she brought a tray with the fresh coffee, *a crescent* and butter to her dear old friend's door and rapped once more.

Sometimes there is something about the end that signals itself, and when Irene drew back the shutters, she wasn't surprised to see that the fingers of Death had crept in before the light. Now there would be not further need to masquerade. The great Actress's longest role had come to an end. The reversed negative in the newspaper decades before had done wonders for her financial stealth and now the old lady could go quietly to her rest under her own name, Vivian de La Roche, past star of the Parisian stage. Her apartment would pass to another fate.

Irene pulled the bedcover over the old lady's head and carried the breakfast tray from the room. Once back in the kitchen, she lifted the receiver from the wall phone and dialed. As the connection went through she leaned her head against the frame of the door to the balcony. A geranium leaf twisting and pivoting into the gusting November wind caught her eye. Suddenly, the leaf gave up it's hold on the stem and was carried on an uplifting draft into the sky. As Irene followed the leafs swirling descent to the street, she began to sob. A voice on the other end of the phone line called her back from her grief.

"*Quel que?*" Melville groggily responded.

"*C'est moi.* It's my old auntie. She has just passed on and I'm here all alone. Can you come and get me?"

"Where I dropped you last week? The old falling-down place on *avenue Salengre?*"

"Yes. That's it. I must call the authorities, so '*revoir.*'"

Melville threw on his clothes. On his way out the door he reached for his helmet but grabbed his leather jacket instead. He bounded down the four flights of stairs and reached his motorbike, covered with a light coat of mist. He wiped the seat with his jacket and unlocked the bike, turned on the ignition and pushed it at a run 'till the motor sputtered to life.

As he approached the corner a half-block away, the semaphore was on warning. Heedlessly, he sped into the intersection.

The driver was looking down at the van's passenger's seat, checking a route list and did not see the motor bike before he slammed it into a traffic plinth.

*   *   *

Paris, the hospital Broussas, off Boulevard Brune, days later

"Tap twice on my hand if you feel this."

The doctor touched a pin to her patient's neck and pushed gently. She felt his fingers tap the back of her hand.

"That's good. That's *very* good, Melville. Now, I want you to try to blow out this candle."

She lit a taper and held the flame near his mouth. He emitted a rasping sound, but the force of his breath wasn't strong enough to put out the flame.

"That's a good try," she said, encouragingly. "Well, keep at it until you can blow it out. You *do want* to do it, don't you, Melville?"

Melville rapped twice on her hand; then twice more.

"Fine. Wanting to do it is practically the same as doing it. The big thing is not giving up. It takes time for the nerves to heal. And some nerves take longer than others. Being able to push the air out has to come before speaking."

*   *   *

The Bar, Le Flanneur, 4th Arrondissement a week afterward

Antoine twisted his aperitif as the two bent over the table.

"But you promised, Bernard, you *promised* fifty-thousand."

"There was one little detail, which is why I wanted to meet you outside of the office."

"Detail? I phoned you as soon as they carted the old bitch away, didn't I?" Bernard stood up, removed a clip of francs from his pocket and placed at ten Franc note under his aperitif glass and leaning both hands over the table, his head inches away from Antoine's and spoke in a low, semi-threatening voice, a tone Antoine had never heard before,

"The detail was, you pathetic *idiot,* is that you killed the wrong old bitch. Now, I want you to lie low for awhile until things cool down."

138

He straightened up and heel-stomped away.

Antoine was stunned-he had never before believed that his close relationship-it had become personal-would devolve into a personal attack, much less one so vehement. He swigged the last of the drink and clenched his jaw and began to think.

*   *   *

Chapter 34

Paris, jardines du Trocadero, the nineteen-eighties

The dachshund tugged his owner through the high hedge-work entryway of the *jardins du Trocadero.* It was early morning, not yet six. Joline LaGrande, was winding down after her morning jog along *rue de Passy* and the grassy park that edged *rue Franklin.* While the run itself had grown increasingly tiring in the past months, she still relished her few minutes in the park, at this time in the morning empty of joggers, dog walkers and service workers short cutting to *Métro Trocadero.* The interlude gave her strength to face her busy day as a partner in one of the *seventh arrondissement's* most exclusive galleries and as owner of a smart club in the *fourth arrondissement.*

The dog, too, found it a high point of his morning while sniffing at traces of the previous day's traffic of people, pets and ground creatures. Somehow he sensed, with the intelligence that humans can't fathom, that he would not see her for perhaps another ten hours, (longer still if she took dinner with friends before returning home), and played animal stunts to prolong the morning romp.

The familiar fretwork of the Eiffel Tower lay beyond an opening in the trees, partly enshrouded in an evanescent fog, yet to evaporate in the daylight. She paused to admire the mist and the play of morning rays on the structure. Against the pressure in her lungs, she drew in the luscious scent of dew-laden evergreens. But, then, the day's schedule intruded on her thoughts. She was to open her gallery half an hour earlier than usual to accommodate an important client, an actress from New York, with whom she would take lunch at *Jules Verne.* From there, she would speed to *Orly* to meet a friend flying in from Berlin.

A tugging at her hand brought her back to the present. The dog, leash fully extended, had disappeared under a thicket of magnolia. "Oh, I haven't time today," she animated. Pulling at the strap she found it taut. Irritated, she pulled again, but it held fast. Crouching down, she duck-walked into the underbrush. The leash had caught on something behind the gnarled trunk of an oak. She squat-walked on, deeper into the brush, pushing aside branches, till she finds behind the tree, her dog's leash entangled with a foot clad in a wine colored sequined pump. Tatters of a shredded silk stocking festooned the macabre setting.

*   *   *

They carried the litter from the underbrush and placed it in the van. The *merlot* dress was as chic as the matching, muddied pumps. One leg fell over the side of the litter and was quickly restored by an attendant.

A small crowd stood casually about, smoking and staring. Cameras clicked. Mutterings from the small gathering,

"Maybe the lady who made the discovery knows something?"

"Who would want to do such a thing?"

"Weird."

"Non c'est pas."

*   *   *

Chapter 35

Paris, Joline LaGrande's apartment, nineteen eighty-two

Joline LaGrande found the small box on her desk when she came in. Tissue-wrapped, not mailed through the post. She poured coffee for herself before parting the tissues and revealing an ivory box and a card. The card was in her assistant Irene's neat hand. In the box was a golden locket. She held it up. Its dulled gold enriched the effect of the octagon's filigree.

"Nice. Very thoughtful. I wonder how she came by it? Felice will love it." She strolled into the bedroom. Felice, already in bed, was reading.

"Something has arrived for you."

"*Moi?*"

"Tonight, something more." She sat on the bedside and proffered the box.

"Not chocolate, either?"

"You haven't been that good."

"Oh, it's lovely. I'll wear it tomorrow night at the club. When I sing *Chantez Moi*, I'll hold it and be singing only to you."

"What about *'J'attendrai'*?"

"I can't wait for you when we've never parted, can I?"

"Nor will we ever."

"Hurry with your bath."

*   *   *

Paris, le Piano Zinc, a late evening

Jean-Baptiste studied the oddly familiar face in the mirror behind the bar, trying to reconcile its features with those of a boy he once knew with the same eyes. He turned to the source of the image and discovered his old schoolmate, Georges, staring back unabashedly. Neither attempted to avert their gaze.

Instead, Jean-Baptiste approached the blue eyes and cleft chin and unselfconsciously slipped his arm about Georges' waist and blurted, at the same time as Georges,

"Let's dance."

And they both began to laugh at the suddenness of their reunion and at their never-before articulated yearnings for each other. They moved to the small, dimly lit floor and danced to Alain's and a snare-drummer's languid rendition of *"J'attendrai."*

Alain continued playing, realizing what was being lost, and that he was powerless to stop what had just occurred so naturally, realizing his own playing was intensifying the rival love that was erasing his own. Yet he continued to play as if he might find in the pain of his loss a torment to replace his passion. His eyes blurred as he saw the two embrace, young fauns in a subtle *pavanne* of passion.

*   *   *

Paris, Irene's apartment in the sixteenth arrondissement, the early nineteen-nineties

The *soirée* at *34, rue de Massenet* included a typical mix of guests: heavy drinkers, more than heavy smokers, sippers, *canapé* hogs, net-workers. Throughout, laughter flowed from room to room above whispered confidences unintentionally overheard by any bystander. And this for two hours before the lights dimmed and the conversations muted as if to blend with the twilight then enfolding with its violet magic the silhouetted roofs beyond the terrace.

Out on the terrace, leaning against the railing, Bernard Foucard was engaged in earnest conversation with a woman of about twenty whose waist matched her age. The two stood close, touching often while looking intently into one another's eyes. From time to time, Bernard flashed a smile and waved his arm expansively over the rooftops, as though describing ownership of all of *Paris*. The woman intermittently punctuated the conversation with chirped responses only a trained canary could imitate. She pushed herself away to the extent of her arm and no farther, while throwing her head back and laughing, tangoing back into his grasp. At length, the two turned towards the roofs beyond. Bernard's arm slipped about her waist and she allowed him to draw her tightly to his side.

Irene Gaspard, meanwhile, passed a tray of baked *canapés* and *pâté*-covered wafers. She smiled as she coaxed her guests to help themselves, but there was something artificial about her mood. She had just seen Bernard's smiling *tête-a-tête* on the terrace. She knew the power of his seductive smile because it had once belonged to her. But, at this shocking instant, she realized it was hers, alone, no more. And while she thought she had left her feelings behind for good, she now found her jealousy-bred grief revived.

"Irene. Irene!" one of the guests was calling to her. It was Fleuraine Grandmont, one of her oldest friends in Paris. Irene did her best to squelch her rising anger.

"You must tell me about the dress. Have I seen it before? I think not. Chanel, I suppose?"

"You jest, *ma chére*. No, a look-alike. A clever Vietnamese seamstress does these things up in the nineteenth. The sequins are hard to sit on at the theater, and you wouldn't believe the problems I had finding the same wine color for the shoes. I gave up hunting and had her do the shoes for me, too. Do you like them?"

"Perfect. Let me know when you want to get rid of them. We do wear the same size, and, frankly, my dear," she cajoled, "the more I think about it, the more I have to say, you look less than stunning in that color."

Fleuraine's chatty comments trailed off when she saw Irene's attention flag and her face lengthen. In all the years they had been friends, Fleuraine had never seen such a haunted look cross Irene's face. She followed her friend's gaze to the terrace and to the couple silhouetted against the dancing lights beyond. And then she understood. Irene was losing Bernard for good. Their little arrangement and its financial rewards might well be at an end. It would never be real Chanels for Irene. And therein lay the shock. A few moments later, like salt on the wound, the couple was upon them.

"Excuse me, Fleuraine. Irene, my dear, Mademoiselle Tavernier has missed the last metro and must get home, so I'm going to drive her. Thanks so much for the splendid evening." He bussed Irene on both cheeks. The young woman, at the prime of her conquest, smiled victoriously as she proffered her hand. Her eyes spirited about the room, omitting her hostess from her view.

Irene took the woman's hand for a moment and then let it fall. She forced a smile as she watched her and Bernard lock arms and disappear through the foyer.

"Well, I'll be," opined Fleuraine. "Of all the nerve."

Irene absently handed her old friend her tray of *canapés*. She had been struck by a chilling surrealistic oeuvre of standing in a glass case which had suddenly shattered.

*   *   *

Chapter 36

Antoine walked from the Trocadero roundabout to the topiaried entrance to the *Jardins du Trocadero*. He paused in the dimming light, uncertain of the layout of the park. He stepped inside the gates, as instructed, and searched for signs to the grotto. Concrete *faux*-entwined vines railed the upward steps.

He had taken but two steps up when he heard Bernard's voice. He turned. "Antoine, over here!"

"Bernie, is that you?"

"Of course, silly one!" The reply was delivered with hoarse insistence.

Antoine moved across the grassy lawn, already damp with early evening dew. He skirted a large shrub to reach Bernard. Bernard embraced him in a bear hug and bussed him on both cheeks. Antoine returned the affection, though taken aback by Bernard's attire.

Bernard pulled away and spoke.

"I'm sorry if I upset you the other evening but there's been a change, dear boy."

"In what you wear on the streets?"

"No, no. Something else. I stopped by your flat this morning-by the way, I've paid the rent for another month-but you wouldn't answer. The old lady at the door said you hadn't left yet?"

Bernard, shifted about, waiting for a comment, but Antoine merely shifted about and lowered his eyes. Bernard continued,

"I didn't have time to wait around. I had three meetings on my calendar. And then I had to get ready for a party that I'm going to tonight. Do you like the costume?" Antoine, somewhat unnerved, replied, "It's, uh, flashy. If I met you on the street, Bernie, I wouldn't recognize you. But why meet at this weird location?"

"I'm going to a party at a social club on the *Troc* and this was convenient. The fact is, your project on Salengre is finished."

"Finished?" Antoine's voice was edged with incredulity. "But I thought as long as the old lady-"

Bernard cut him short.

"The old bitch is dead, as you know and no thanks to you, saving me a lot of trouble. I'm bringing in a different crew, one that works better. I tried to 'phone you to tell you, and when I couldn't reach you last night, I went to your flat this morning and —."

"But I know the project, Bernie. You told me so yourself. But that's nothing. What's to become of ... us?"

"Actually, there never was much of an *us,* Antoine, except in your mind. There's the age difference and ... I would have told you sooner, but..."

"Merde!" Antoine burst out.

"Merde! MERDE! You told me you cared for me, Bernie! I *believed* you!" Antoine shouted and sobbed.

"I did once, at the beginning. But things change. But cheer up! I've gotten a job for you. In Lille and a little bit extra. Starting next month. You can keep the clothes, of course."

Bernard handed an envelope to Antoine, whose features were becoming taut with anger.

"Did you bring the Lugar?"

Antoine, tearing away the wrapper, pulled out a one-thousand franc note. He fingered inside the envelope for more. Finding nothing, he let the envelope fall to the ground. He stared at Bernard, barely able to control his sobs.

"Yes. But a thousand francs. A thousand fucking francs! Is that what I am worth to you, Bernie? Here's your fucking Lugar. It's not loaded. See?" He aimed the gun towards Bernard's head and pulled the trigger and stomped out of the garden, still sobbing. "A thousand francs. *A thousand fucking francs!*"

Moments later, on the roadway, just opposite, a car door slammed and a sedan purred off into the night, Antoine at the wheel.

*　　*　　*

Chapter 37

The gallery LaGrande, the next morning

Joline was nowhere to be seen at the gallery in the morning, nor that afternoon. Irene was not disappointed that her employer, this woman of many disguises, had not yet appeared. When the phone rang, she answered it reluctantly, hoping it wasn't she.

"Inspector Dubufet. May I speak with Mademoiselle Irene Gaspard?"

"I am she, Inspector… Inspector…"

"Dubufet, Mademoiselle. There is a matter at the *Gardens du Trocadero*. We would like you to assist us."

"Nothing serious, I hope. I hardly know the area. Where is your office? I can take a taxi."

"That won't be necessary. I'll send a car for you. To the gardens. *Au revoir*, Mademoiselle."

"*Au revoir*, Monsieur Inspecteur."

Irene set down the receiver. Her face reflected her bewildered concern.

*   *   *

Paris, les jardins du Trcadero, that same afternoon

"Mademoiselle Gaspard, thanks for coming. We need your help. A body has been found. It won't be pleasant. I'm going to lift the cover here and I just need you to tell me if this person is known to you. Are you ready?"

"I guess so, Monsieur Inspector."

"It's very strange. This is nearly the spot from where we carried a mannequin, dressed the same way, some weeks ago. Would you know the connection?"

"About that, yes, Monsieur Inspector. I'm a bit ashamed. I hope I won't get into trouble. But at the time, she wasn't too popular with the people in her shop. She didn't treat them very well. It was late. We had a game. We dressed the mannequin and hid it here.

"It was all terribly hilarious at three in the morning when we were getting ready for a big opening and were all drunk. I can see now it wasn't so amusing. But no one would have harmed her...perhaps just to frighten her on her morning dog walk."

"Perhaps if you would look at the remains." He bent down and pulled away the plastic shroud.

Irene shuddered as she viewed the macabre inventory: the *merlot* sequined dress, form-fitting; one silk stocking, tattered, partially covering the crimson sequined pump. The only piece missing from the mordant tableaux was her little dog. And Joline LaGrande, herself. For sheathed in the dress was not the director of *Gallerie LaGrande* and doyenne of the *Club Joline*, but Bernard Foucard, with a .38 millimeter umber hole burnt into the center of his forehead, the blood having dried to the same color of the dress.

"So, he had a private life, after all. And a flair for matching colors," she mused to herself.

"Would you have any idea who would have done this to your employer?" Irene thought furiously but remained outwardly calm. Now was her chance. Finally. Deliciously. It was time to squash that snake, Antoine. The one who had taken not only her innocence on the potting shed floor but took much more, repeatedly; the one who threatened to tell her parents when she got pregnant; the one who deceptively drew her to *Montparnasse* station for a final abandonment, the serial betrayals leading to venomous hatred, welled up and, now, about to be unleashed. Remaining outwardly casual as a school girl asking for street directions of a policeman she fixed an innocent look on her face, one that had done her much service since her fifth school form.

"I didn't know much about Bernard's business. I was only a secretary in the office, two or three days a week, doing what I was told, not making any of the decisions, lucky to have a job. But I kept a record of some of his phone calls, in case he needed them. Oh, come to think of it, there *was* a strange man who came in recently. Only once. I heard Bernard tell him, when he thought they were alone, not to come to the office again and that they had 'to be careful'. I hope it's alright for me to be telling you this because I wouldn't want to get anyone in trouble. I think I have the man's number, though." She fumbled in her purse for her black book. She recited a telephone number from its back pages. The inspector thanked her and told her the police car would take her back to work. As she turned away the Inspector followed her, extending some keys in his hands.

"Mademoiselle, you were on friendly terms with Monsieur Foucard, no? Any problems?"

"We've known each other for some time. He hired me when I first came to *Paris*. We were on good terms."

"Mademoiselle, I believe these may be yours." As he came close, he playfully dangled the key-ring from his outstretched hand.

"They were found by the earlier body discovery, some months ago. Your initials are on the tag. We have no further use for them."

She took the keys, thanked him, turned and got into the car.

*　　*　　*

Outside *les Jardins du Trocadero,* the dachshund tugged at the leash, wanting to go in. Joline LaGrande, lacking the stamina for a longer walk, pulled him away, saying, "not today; it's late; tomorrow, if you're good." The dog pulled the leash towards the hedge and lifted his leg. She stared vacantly towards the tower, then moved to a nearby bench and drew out a cigarette and lit it, drawing in a deep breath and exhaling as the dog finished his business. A spasm of coughing caused her to stub out the cigarette and leave the bench and walk homeward, the dog happily scampering right and left in momentary explorations: grasses, stones, things that only dogs place behind human ken.

*　　*　　*

Chapter 38

Paris, the Club Joline, a few weeks later

He dropped the telephone receiver back into the cradle, Stunned, he wanted at first not to think about it. But he realized he would have do something. He ran to the dressing room door and shouted,

"Felice, Felice! It's the hospital. It's..."

Felice came to the door while still adjusting her performance dress. It was nearly time for her entrance. She looked quizzically at Jean-Babtiste and turned her back on him. "Zip me up, please and calm down. Tell me what this is all about."

*   *   *

Val de Grace Hospital, a few hours later

Joline LaGrande tried to catch the words being whispered at the foot of her bed. The utterances of the doctors and new visitors made no sense to her. When she caught the sound of a familiar voice, though, she opened her eyes and rasped,

"Jean-Babtiste, Jean-Babtiste."

Though exhausted and breathing labouredly, she felt she had to make the effort. When he came to kneel at her bedside, she could only see his father Sargan's features-the chin, the wide-set eyes. The narcotics loosened her will and she struggled to form her words, finding it difficult to gasp out the syllables. Groping with her emotions, even in her narcotic state, uncertain as to what she should reveal, what was she should not reveal, right, what was not right. In her confused state, she whispered only part of the truth.

He held her hand until it relaxed.

*   *   *

Paris, the Club Joline, soon after

Felice Jouillard stood at the curve of the piano. She wore a black sheath. Around her neck hung the octagonal gold locket. Alain improvised his segue from the previous number as she found more words.

"These songs have been about Joline, her life and her loves. Now, I want to share with you her last musical moment, before she left us, forever. It's an American song, perhaps her all-time favorite, called 'Everytime We Say Goodbye.'"

The lights dimmed as Felice began her last song to Joline LaGrande. Random rays glancing off the revolving crystal ball struck the locket, beaming off future dreams into the lives of listeners for whom a first love would at that very moment begin.

*   *   *

Chapter 39

In and around Roscoff, the following days

The autobus chugged through the evening fog enveloping the artichoke fields. Occasionally, it stopped to let off students returning to their homes for a school holiday. From inside the bus, Jean-Baptiste stared vacantly as the road snaked through the mustard-colored hills mutating from lavender to deep purple as dusk settled in. He was only half-aware of what he saw: the roads, the fields, the reflection of the interior of the bus, his own face in the glass. His thoughts were with Felice, still in *Paris,* and with Georges at his side.

When the autobus stopped in the parking lot at the foot of the path leading to *Roscoff's* small casino, Jean-Baptiste and Georges alit with their small packs. Jean-Baptiste had hoped he would remember the streets, but he was in a dream as the autobus disappeared along the rock wall canyon that surrounded the village.

They headed toward the sea, eventually following the road which hugged the harbor. Where the road curved in front of *l'Auberge Gaspard*, they found a perch on the seawall and sat back-to-back. Georges retrieved sandwiches from his pack. He handed one over his shoulder to Jean-Baptiste. Silently, they ate as the darkness closed in and the tide washed the small boats in the harbor till they tipped upright and floated. A door in the hotel opened and the Gaspard's old pet, *Roué*, ambled arthritically over. He nuzzled Jean-Baptiste and put his head on the young man's lap. His tail flopped several times and grew still. The harbor light soon swung its protective beam across the horizon. As the two friends fell asleep, the red boat, urged out of its sandy nest, pulled at its anchor chain.

∗   ∗   ∗

The next morning at the Hospital Saint-Jude on the outskirts of *Roscoff* Melville Saint-Eustace sat up in his bed. Irene Gaspard, at his side, held the mouth of a bottle to his mouth. He blew, creating a steamboat-like whistle.

"Que marveilleux, Melville," Irene exclaimed as she looked to the physician standing nearby for confirmation. The physician shrugged his shoulders and shook his head negatively. Irene constrained a sob as she turned toward the window.

*　　*　　*

In his unheated attic near the harbor, Sargan Gaspard arose from his bed. Fits of coughing and a pain in his left arm had kept him awake most of the night. He stepped to the dormer window. Searing pain shot upward into his chest. His blurred vision of the harbor veered into the blackness of death as he slumped to the floor.

At *le cimetiére de Sainte-Agnes,* a somber cluster of mourners braced themselves against the early morning chill. A small military band sounded, in a fashion, *"La Marseillaise"* to send Louise Vernet's spirit out to sea.

In the official garb of one of France's highest dignitaries — a black overcoat, a silk hat. The ribbon of the Legion of Honor pinned to his lapel — the government's representative pressed the copy of his eulogy to the lectern as brisk *Breton* winds tried to pull it from his grasp.

"The President of France and all her people are saddened by the death of Louise Vernet, heroine of the Resistance, unjustly tried near these same shores for treason she did not commit. Louise Vernet put her life in the hands of the enemy in order to fight bravely for justice, for freedom, and for France. From humble beginnings on a farm nearby, she advanced with the aid of her innate nobility, her steadfastness, and her unstinting bravery. She carried on day by day in her secret missions for the Resistance. She carried on through hours and sometimes days of torture. And through the regrettable indignities shamefully cast upon her by the country that she strove to serve, she carried on. Now, on behalf of the President of France, the French people and the cause of freedom, I bestow on Louise Vernet France's highest honor. Her name will be inscribed in the *Madeleine* among those we hold most hallowed."

Another dignitary handed over a silver trowel, glancing about, taking in what to him had once been a familiar view. August Martin Bernard Eduard Friedlander, previously a native of Munich and in the Second World War, a Colonel in the SS, had brought some of his forgery skills to the fore during the chaotic last days of the Parisian evacuation, remaining secluded in a Parisian apartment owned by the elderly aunt of *Roscoff's* premier citizen, Alois Castaignet. Through further artisanship, he had secured an appointment as antiquarian in charge of restoring looted French antiquities, carried away in the war. His superiors in the post-war government were impressed by the knowledge that he seemed to intuit concerning the whereabouts of skillfully hidden artifacts.

Handing the silver trowel to the senior official, he removed his silk hat and bowed his head as the official intoned,

"This earth, this part of France that she so loved and which betrayed her, will cover her once-vibrant remains. France now returns her to honor."

As he spoke the last words, he doffed his hat and bent to the grave and, with the trowel, stabbed the wet earth, lifting a clod of the Breton soil, allowing the wind sprinkle it upon the casket. A snare drum beat a quiet tattoo as Louise Vernet, a heroine of France, was lowered to her last resting place. The band again trumpeted *"la Marseillaise."* The dignitary replaced his silk hat, and the assemblage walked with bowed heads past the graves of Alois Castaignet and Fleur Saint-Eustace to the cemetery gate.

At the rear of the cemetery, the harsh winds pulled at the cover of the cardboard box, buried by Louise's unwitting informant, Klaus Berwald, before his soldier's death. The gusts pulled at the box's now-rotted lid, flipped it open, and lifted aside a damp layer of Swiss francs. Drier bills, suddenly released, took flight, at first blowing after the retreating cortege and then disappearing like hundreds of swallows into the clouds above the sea. Friedlander, glancing up at the money in flight, thought to himself,

"So that's where he hid it." A rueful smile crept across his face.

So engrossed with the flight of the money as he filed back to his official car, the second of the procession that he did not notice another sedan, one with the discreet markings of the *Sûreté,* nearby.

A mustachioed officer in plain clothes advanced with three uniformed police at his side.

"Sir, you are Deputy Ambrose Sonomme?"

"Of course. Who do I have the honor to meet?"

"Inspector in Chief, Louis Jourdain, *Sûreté.* I would like to have a word with you about some affairs at *Drancy,* during the Second War, Colonel Friedlander. Come with us."

Standing on the cemetery steps Sarah Goldschmidt, in a fur trimmed coat, advanced towards the automobile. Inspector Jordain took notice of her and held the others back from entering the car.

"Madame Goldschmidt!"

"*Bon Jour*, Monsieur le Chief Inspector."

Turning to Friedlander her facial features ambienced granite as she pulled out black corduroy jacket, upon which she had sewn a yellow Star of David. She held out the jacket, shaking it as she spoke.

"Of course you recognize the jacket. I embroidered the collar for my brother, Isaiah in 'forty-two, before you took him off to be killed. Here, you can have it back; no decent Frenchman would wear it."

So saying, she flung the jacket to Friedlander's feet and went to a waiting car the door being held open. She entered the car, the door slammed and the car sped off. Sarah Goldschmidt had had her moment. Even so, random thoughts raced through her mind: memories of her family in the *Marais;* their somber loading into the transport buses; the arrogant tilt of Friedlander's jaw as he stood by; the memory of Friedlander's false identity card view through her cousin's microscope; Friedlander as "Ambrose Sonomme", the pupils of his eyes in triumphant glare, contrived as miniature swastikas. She thought of the nameless, starved concentration camp genius who delivered up Friedlander and others. As her car sped through the mist toward Paris, she leaned forward and buried her face in her hands, sobbing out the *Kaddish* in final tears for her parents and their lost dreams, her brother's jacket lying with her memories, discarded in the puddle at the cemetery gate.

*   *   *

As Catherine Gaspard prepared the morning buffet for her guests, she saw from out of the kitchen window, as if suspended in the harbor mist, two figures sleeping back-to-back on the harbor wall. She couldn't pinpoint what drew her to them but she found herself suddenly flying to the front door of the hotel. She was already on the street before she caught herself and forced herself to reflect. Roué was suddenly at her side, wagging his tail and barking. She ventured hesitantly across the road and then swung her arms wide and began to call out. "Jean Baptiste! Jean Baptiste!" She knelt down, sobbing, clasping in her arms the blonde young man she knew to be her lost boy. In the harbor, the Red Boat, free of its mooring, the golden sun splashing its hull, drifted out to the open sea.

"*J'attendrai*" wafted from a distant radio.